Title Page

Copyright Page

Table of Contents

Chapter 1: Pledging

"Pledges! March!"

Everything was dark. The blindfolds were supposed to scare us or hide something. I didn't feel any fear, only curiosity crossed my mind.

My hand rested on the shoulder in front of me, just like the guy behind me had his hand resting on my shoulder. Several of us were in sequential order and walking in unison. It was quiet enough to hear things that usually go unnoticed.

I felt our steps following a declining path as the smell of burnt grass began infiltrating the atmosphere. The horrendous smell of ash eclipsed everything else and choked us up. Our hands were tied, so we had to cough on the necks and backs in front of us. At that moment, I wished to be in the back of the line.

The smoke became denser with each step we took. Once smoke filled my lungs, a deep voice yelled, "Halt! Face forward! State your pledge names."

It was Antoine King, president of the Gamma Alpha Gamma fraternity. The first pledge stepped forward, then yelled, "Chicken, cluck-cluck, shiettt!"

The next pledge stepped forward, and blurted out, "Fire, bang bang bang, cracker!"

I knew that voice. It was my boy, Dustin. He was the only white boy brave and soulful enough to try pledging to a black fraternity. Being himself made him accepted.

The line of pledges continued as each one announced their respective name. I was toward the back of the line, so the buildup was intense. Suddenly, I heard the pledge before me end his intro. I stepped up next.

I yelled, "Dora!" Then clapped my hands on my elbows, chest, and shoulders, in alignment with all the swag of the next Gamma superstar. My hands came together, shaped like a book. Then I shouted, "Winifred Reeeeaddd!" and dragged my book hands in front of my face slowly as I said the word read.

I had the most embarrassing pledge name of everyone. Don't get me wrong, Chicken Crap is trash, and a redheaded white man referring to himself as

Firecracker was just plain cruel, but Dora Winifred Read? They made me go by the name of Arthur's little sister from the children's show. Out of all the cartoon characters, D.W. Read! They did me dirty.

At least those other names were creative. They gave me the name because my initials - DW and name, Dagobert Waller. They couldn't have been more creative than that?

"Hoods down!" Antoine commanded. We removed our hoods one by one, revealing ourselves. He continued, "Blindfolds off!" We removed our blindfolds, to see a crowded setting. It seemed like the whole school was here. I frantically gazed across the people in the crowd as applause roared.

My gaze settled on a beautiful woman. She was as fine of a woman as a man could see. She blessed my eyes which should have been shrouded by the darkness I experienced for hours. Her skin was smooth and dark. Her lips were full, her hair was short, and her eyes were brown with long lashes and dark eye shadow. This woman was one of a kind. As she brushed the baby hairs from her forehead, she exposed the butterfly tattoo on her right wrist. She was thin and dressed to impress in a sun dress.

Nakia Taylor was the reason I decided to pledge Gamma Alpha Gamma. She had a way of convincing a fool like me to do anything. As my pledge initiation began, I couldn't help but admire the woman who helped get me here. She made eye contact with me and smiled with her florescent white teeth.

Our mutual gaze was interrupted by a glare from a heavy, muscular light-skinned brother, who stood across from me. His cat eyes stared into my soul. He was my only line brother more muscular than me. Jermaine was 6 feet 8, 285 pounds, and a star lineman on the football team.

Antione shouted, "Pledges! Welcome to the start of the rest of your lives. Let me make one thing clear. No one here is special. You are all average. Actually, you're worse than average. You're…"

Antoine looked over to DeDe, another fraternity leader, and paused. Then proudly said, "Allow me to introduce Brother DeDe Brooks. Your Pledge Master for the remainder of the semester." Antoine stepped back as the light-skinned brother stepped forward.

"Pledges! Gamma creed, now!" DeDe yelled. He sounded like a cartoon or Mickey Mouse Clubhouse type of brother.

We recited the gamma creed in unison - "Love. For All. Love. For Education. Love. For soul. Love for my brothers. Love. Gammas!"

Dede smirked, then said, "I'm going to enjoy being y'all daddy. Now, break! Meet at the house by midnight and no one better be late!"

After small talk with a few friends, I began trying to find Nakia in the crowd. None of this would have been possible without her supporting me throughout the whole process.

Once I greeted her, I dramatically said, "Now, how are you going to show up here looking like that? You know I have to concentrate for the rest of the semester, and nothing distracts me like you in a sundress."

Nakia playfully said, "Shut up big head! With everything going on in my life, you think I'm worried about distracting you?"

We hugged, and then I responded, "I'm playing with you, but in all seriousness, I appreciate everything you've done for me. If it wasn't for you pushing me to pledge Gamma, I have no idea where I'd be right now."

Her vanilla scent and graceful essence made me realize there was no place I would have rather been.

When she assured me that I could always count on her, she changed the topic and said, "Tonight I have to give a speech downtown about Terrence Grey. I need to get the African American community energized and informed. It's time we strategize to mobilize. And we can't do that until we all recognize. The only way for our voices to be heard is for us to make them heard!"

I watched her beauty as the passion emitted from her eyes. On top of those looks, she always had an elegant, poetic choice of words. Not to mention, her love for social justice and racial equality. Those weren't my focuses, but she made me think twice about them. After continuously nodding she continued, "My speech tonight will prepare our community for the protests. We need to push the next senator to make changes. Whether it's Senator Avery or Senator Martinsville, the next white man in office better give a damn about black people!"

I didn't know what to add to the conversation, so I asked, "Who are you voting for?"

Her eyes widened and she answered, "Who am I voting for? Who am I voting for? You really don't know a damn thing about politics, do you?"

I dismissively said, "It doesn't matter. They're all rich white folks to me." While I playfully fueled Nakia's fire, Dede interjected and said, "Excuse me. Pledges aren't allowed to joke around, especially with the pledge master's girl." It felt like an insult to injury when they kissed after he tried putting me in my place.

I tried lightening the mood by extending my hand and saying, "It's nothing like that my brother. Nakia is my homegirl, that's it. We just be doing our thing sometimes."

He left me hanging to solidify the embarrassment, then said, "Pledge Dora Winifred Read, I don't think you quite understand who you are talking to. First and foremost, you will never refer to me as brother. Not as long as you remain a pledge. Secondly, there will be no more 'doing your thing' when it comes to Nakia, got it?"

"Wha…" I laughed and looked over at Nakia, then back at homeboy, and continued my statement, "You kidding right?"

He stepped toward me and asked, "Does my countenance display the slightest bit of humor to you?"

I shook my head and waved bye to Nakia.

As I walked away, I noticed DeDe's frustration build. Nakia tried to calm him down, but I could tell he was still trying to get something off his chest. Then, he let those words out - "You lucky she vouched for you bitch!"

My blood began boiling when I asked him to repeat his statement. Our massive bodies sandwiched Nakia as she tried to de-escalate the situation. He stood on business and reiterated, "I called you a bitch!" Our faces were centimeters apart. Once we felt each other's breaths on our noses, he barked, "And if you want to remain a pledge of the Gamma Alpha Gamma fraternity, a female dog is exactly what you will be to your pledge master. You understand that bitch?"

I wanted to whip this bitch ass dude so bad until he couldn't remember his own name. However, I bit my tongue and took this L on the chin. I muttered, "Understood. I'll see you later Nakia."

Pride is a hard pill to swallow. Something like taking those pills when you go to a foreign country. Being a military brat, I had to do that a lot. My brothers Morris and Sinclair and I were always traveling with our pops growing up. I still miss those days.

When I reconnected with Dustin and my roommate Skittles, they had no clue what I just experienced. It felt like only the people I was pledging with knew what we were going through. Even then, all of us had our own unique struggles.

"Well, what do we have here?" A familiar, wormy voice said, "Ole Dago the bum and the clumsy white friends." A lanky light, light-skinned guy named Raphael with a curly high-top fade slid through, rubbing his hands as his stooge snickered alongside him.

"I may be white, but at least I ain't stupid, Raphael", Dustin clapped back with a juvenile response like he always did.

"Good one mayonnaise. Don't make me have my boy here handle you." He smacked his sidekick on the chest as he flashed his florescent smile, rubbing his hands together after.

"I'll throw down right now!" Dustin thrusted his arms around like a kid.

"You talking a lot, Raphael," I held Dustin back. "Nigga got a 2.3 GPA. The only reason you're pledging Gamma is cuz you're so far up DeDe's behind; he got you wiping too." I slapped hands with Dustin as we laughed.

"You funny Dago," Raphael hissed. "Ain't he funny Sway?"

"Hilarious," his little stooge said without any emotion on his face.

"Damn, if Sway thinks you are funny, then you are real funny," Raphael continued. "But we ain't come here for jokes. We came here for a proposition."

"Man, if you don't get out of here with your jerry curly fade," I joked as Dustin and I slapped hands again. Ole Fresh Prince of Belair wannabe!

"Again, you funny Dago." No emotion on Raphael's face. "Do me a favor and put the clown crap aside homie. I'm stepping to you like a man now." His eyes scanned my homies up and down. "You know you can't stick with these fools when you are pledging Gamma, bro. You a real one, Dago. But if you wanna achieve with the Gammas, you gotta roll with us. I got all the secrets to succeeding, fam."

"What, fool!" Dustin yelled as I held him back.

I felt Dustin's energy loud and clear. He was ready to fight anyone over pride. Skittles had been uncharacteristically quiet since Raphael and little homie got here. Strange.

"Hold on Dustin," I pushed my dude back with the bone of my knuckle. "What secrets you got Raphael? How to fail a semester in 1 week?"

"Got plenty of secrets D Dub and none of them involve failure." His eyes studied me like he was trying to read my thoughts. "I know some secrets about why you really got chosen to pledge Gamma too and something about your history, that you don't even know."

My history? This man better step if he wanna step.

"I got chosen to pledge Gamma for two reasons. Real and One. You're a clown bro. Give us the so-called secret or move on out."

"Let's just say I got all the answers for tonight's test, and believe me when I say it ain't no easy A".

"Man, if you don't get outta here we gonna kick your easy A," Dustin blurted out."

"What do you say, D Dub?" Raphael asked while ignoring Dustin's rage. "Are you ready to roll with me and the wolves on the path to Gamma greatness? Maybe find out a little bit about yourself before the brothers want you to."

"You know, I would. But you are more like a sheep in wolves clothing, homie. Putting on an act to impress daddy DeDe." That pissed him off. "I'm loyal to my boys." I dapped Dustin up. Skittles was still in his own little world.

"Fine," Raphael said before stepping to my face, inches away. He's just like his daddy DeDe. "But be warned homie. You ain't getting no other chance. And as soon as you and your crew catch a whiff of what the Gammas have in store for us tonight… you'll be crawling to me, begging to ride with us."

"Word. I'll let you know when that happens, so you got some extra time to pull that big head outta daddy DeDe's doo doo."

"Let's rock Sway," he told his stooge with his eyes still stuck on mine. "Awooo," he howls like the fool he is. "Wolves baby." Raphael and Sway faded away like that corny haircut he had.

"Can you believe that clown, D Dub?" Dustin asked.

I ain't never gonna step on my dudes. But a part of me wants to know what Raphael meant by my history. Skittle laughed and said, "He does have a point when it comes to you, Dustin."

"Boy, if you don't shut up with that," Dustin threw his head back and smacked his lips.

I laughed at the two of them. Are these really the people Raphael wanted me to abandon? Hell nah. The humor alone kept me around. But my laughter was cut short when my phone buzzed. It was a message from my brother Sinclair.

Chapter 2: My Brother's Keeper

Once I returned inside, I locked up behind me and pulled my laptop out. I was always nervous whenever I hopped on a video call with my brother Sinclair. He may have been younger than me, but he had it all together. He's the most studious guy I knew. My family always thought he was the chosen one and would be the one to make something of himself. They were right. He was in med school, killing it.

"What's up big bro!" Sinclair exclaimed as he appeared on the screen. He looked so much like my older brother, Morris, aside from his grandma glasses.

I warmly greeted him, "My guy! You are looking like Doctor Waller today man. Ease up on them kid! How have you been?"

Sinclair had always been the grandmaster of cornballs and I wasn't shy about letting him know it. However, if anyone else picked on him, Morris and I would be the first to address it.

He responded, "I've been good big bro! We do a lot of cool things in the lab out here. Today, we looked at some clinical benefits from a range of microscopic lifeforms. Tomorrow we're studying a family of fungi known as Cladosporium Sphaerosperum. They're able to grow with toluene as a full source of carbon."

I interjected, "Damn, that's crazy!" To pretend I cared.

He smiled even wider because he didn't sense the sarcasm and continued, "I know bro and that's not even the craziest part! Get this! Cladosporium Sphaerosperum is a radiotrophic fungi. That means they can use radiation as an energy source to stimulate growth. Imagine the endless possibilities in the medical field!"

I added another, "Damn, that's crazy."

The he added, "I'm thinking of doing some research on it. Other than that, I've just been busy studying. I got my first USMLE coming up next month. The grind's been real bro. I need to ace my residency application. I've literally been studying for this all year."

His goal reminded me of how far he made it. I smiled and said, "You know moms is proud of you right? When is the last time you talked to her?"

My brother's demeanor shifted downward and said, "Just before I texted you. She's worried about you bro. You should call her."

An awkward silence took over the call. When Sinclair waited for me to break it, I responded, "Nah. I ain't got nothing to say to her. Me grinding in college is enough for her. I'll take care of her once I make something of myself, but me and her ain't never gonna be good again."

My brother put some tone in his voice and said, "You have to stop blaming her for dad bro."

I deflected, "How's the love life little bro? Are there any fine doctors out that way? I bet your med school is crawling with them. Some bad nurses too."

He stood up and said, "Dagobert, we are going to have to talk about this someday. Dad's death wasn't mom's fault. He was in the military. He had many enemies!"

I failed at suppressing my emotions and flashed out, "Stop it bro! I don't blame mom for pops. I blame her for Morris! When dad was reported dead, moms knew she had no way of making money. So, she pushed Morris to the limit. That was my big bro! He taught me how to play football. We were supposed to make it to the league together She pushed Morris so hard that he lost his love for the game. That caused him to disappear. Of course, I blame mom! You weren't close with Morris like I was. That's why you can talk to mom every day like nothing's wrong! You always been a mama's boy!"

His apology for bringing it up didn't do anything to calm my nerves. I was tired of acting like everything was all good. It wasn't and I was tired of playing like it was. My brother and I rarely talked because of his studies and blind affiliation with our mother. She had the wool over his eyes about who she really was.

Chapter 3: Kintinge Night

Lightning struck as the dark cloudy sky prepared to rain down on our New Orleans college town. The Gamma House rested at the top of the tallest hill in town. From up there, I could see the whole city and bayous. Unfortunately, I couldn't enjoy the view. Not after that crap with Sinclair. Plus, I was too busy looking at the ugly gargoyle statue next to me. The Gamma house had plenty of things that gave me the creeps.

The crib was like a castle. My pledge brothers and I sat by the front lawn of the house. The Greek letters Gamma Alpha Gamma decorated the face of the palace written in gold. The architecture spoke volumes about their legacy and money.

"Y'all ready for this? The real work starts tonight!" Raphael yelled as he cuffed his mouth with both hands. He walked amongst the herd of pledges, trying to hype up the crowd.

We had 40 pledges in total. I stood among them, studying the crowd and envisioning them becoming my brothers. Dustin asked, "What y'all think they gonna have us doing tonight?"

I responded, "I heard they gonna make us do the elephant walk." Fear filled Jameson's face. He may have been the peppiest person on campus.

Before they could ask more questions, Dede and two other brothers emerged through the front doors wearing the Gamma purple, green, and yellow colors representing the fraternity. Dede led the other two, who were carrying blindfolds. He demanded for us to put them on while he angrily locked eyes with me.

DeDe and his crew led us in a single file line. I felt the hardness of the marble floor on the bottom of my sneakers as we entered the Gamma House. Suddenly, loud music thundered. The beat of electronic bass rattled my mind.

When someone can't see, their other senses are heightened. The music moved through my body like a pulse. They were playing, *Wild For the Night* by A$AP Rocky. Dede demanded for us to remove our blindfolds. I slowly retracted the cloth from my face and was surprised by what I saw.

Brothers of Gamma Alpha Gamma were rocking their letters everywhere. Drinks floated around in red, purple, green, and yellow plastic cups. There were more bad honeys than I ever saw in my life. They were dancing and having a good time. The finest ones were by the DJ booth. The DJ had the crib rocking. His style reminded me of the hottest disk jockey I knew - DJ Plaque. Matter of fact, it was DJ Plaque. He was always overbooked, and many saw him as the best DJ in the city.

Antione approached me holding a red cup and a fine woman on his arms, then said, "My brother, the Gammas have access to entertainers you wouldn't possibly believe." Dede walked up at the same time and said, "Pledge Dora Winifred Read!" I jumped like a cricket as he slid next to Antoine. He extended his hand and said, "Relax boy. I'm sorry we got off on the wrong foot. I'm just a little protective of my girl."

I conceded, "It's all good homie. I would be the same way if I had a girl like Nakia. But trust me man, we've only been friends for a long time."

Our beef was over when he handed me a drink and responded, "I got you, brother. You don't have to worry about me coming at you anymore. I'm here to help you in any way I can." He raised his voice and shouted to the room, "And that goes for all y'all! This party is for y'all! Welcome to Kintinge night!"

Cheers erupted from the brothers as DJ Plaque played 90's hip-hop tunes on the boards. My drink tasted like a fruit roll-up and a woman just my type approached me as the music sped up. This party gave off a vibe like no other and was a beautiful break from everyday life.

When Dustin and I noticed another girl staring at me, he encouraged me to approach her. She was standing with someone of rank in the fraternity. Apollo was the fraternity treasurer. It was rumored that DeDe beat him out for the pledge master position and that Apollo had to settle for another spot. The girl he was with had a face and body that could stop traffic. Nonetheless, I didn't want to get myself into any more trouble, so I resisted going holler at her.

Despite my hesitation to connect with her, that didn't stop us from connecting. She approached me and called me by my nickname – D Dub. When I asked how she knew my other alias, she smirked and responded, "Everyone's been talking about you. You played running back for the football team. Your brother was Morris Waller, wasn't he? He almost went pro and has a lot of history around here."

Nothing retracted my attraction away faster than her mentioning Morris. I took a sip of my drink and silently walked away. She pled, "I didn't mean to make you upset. I am so sorry. I'll see you around and we can start over then. My name is Diamond and don't you forget it."

I was being tested in real time. I knew she was off limits, but she made sure I thought of her even after she made me mad. Her attention made me want to become a Gamma brother even more so.

As she disappeared, I saw Nakia storming through the crowd and running outside while crying tears. Her distraught presence triggered something in me and sobered me up. I chased after her and shoved my way through the party. When I reached the backyard, I saw DeDe chasing after his girl.

He yelled her name and grabbed her wrist, then asked, "What on earth are you upset about, woman?"

Her eyes watered, and her body trembled because he was clueless. Nakia gave him several moments to figure it out. When he didn't, she yelled, "Don't play dumb you fool! You know exactly why I'm upset. You promised to be at my speech tonight."

DeDe threw his head back and responded, "Is that really what this is about? Your speech? You do realize that this is our Kintinge Night for the pledges? Do you have any idea what that means for the fraternity?" Tears streamed down her face, and she exclaimed, "Do you have any idea what my speech means for the community, black people, and me?"

He lowered his tone and said, "I understand clearly Nakia, but I have duties as a leader to my Fraternity." Her tone went in the opposite direction. Nakia yelled back, "What about your duties as a black man?" Things appeared as if they were about to get physical, but that didn't scare Nakia. She stepped toward her boyfriend and said, "DeDe, you're beginning to really make me question who I chose to be with. You got the swag, the bag, and the overwhelming tendency to brag. You're strong, long, and know how to write a love song, but baby you will never keep a woman like me until you realize when you're wrong." Nakia was out of his sight before he could respond and before they could witness me watching.

All of me wanted to find Nakia and comfort her. Seeing her cry like that twisted my insides. However, I couldn't abandon my pledging duties and disappear on Kintinge Night.

After using the bathroom, I ran into Diamond again. Once we locked eyes, I asked her if she was trying to get me kicked out of the fraternity. "I don't want you out," she said as her fingers traced my chest. I caught a chill, then whispered, "We're not doing this." She ignored my helpless whisper and led me behind closed doors.

Chapter 4: Meet the Gammas

Lust got the best of me. I tried blending back into the party. Moments after rejoining the party, I began losing all functionality, my vision became blurry, and I started drooling. My world went black until I reopened my eyes butt naked in a ditch.

The first thing I saw was Jermaine, naked and beaten up just like me. I fully regained consciousness when Dede spoke through the megaphone and said, "Gentleman, welcome to your first challenge. The beginning of a long schedule of efforts to prove you are down for us. To prove you can hang with us. To prove you are Gamma material! Most of you failed your test during Kintinge night. Y'all proved too belligerent to stay sober. Most of y'all are still drunk. I commend those of you who kept your composure. You showed restraint and responsibility. The true measure of a Gamma man. This will help you with this challenge. We dug 20 ditches. In each ditch, two of you stand across from each other. Look at your pledge brother. This is the last time you will look at this person as a pledge brother. Gentlemen, the 20 ditches represent 20 pledges. That is the maximum number of pledges the Gammas will be initiating this semester. On my mark, you will fight the person across from you. Man to man. No one is allowed to leave the ditch until a winner is decided. The loser gets dropped and the winner moves on with us. The fight is over when one person is either knocked out or has tapped out."

White lights blasted from all directions, heating my skin. I was blinded momentarily, but as the initial shock faded, I could make out the setting. Jermaine and I stood naked in a 10-foot ditch. Over top, Gamma brothers cheered, howled, and honked their horns."

"I like you D Dub, but ima tear your butt up boy. I was born to be Gamma!"

Before I knew it, I was pinned down and spitting blood. He wrapped his arms around me and shoved me to the ground.

I pushed myself off the dirt, just to be punched in the jaw again. This time, he knocked a tooth out. I spit it out and was ready to counter him. Momentum shifted when I heard others cheering for him.

They wanted this and DeDe wanted this. He set me up to fail. As I get my butt kicked, I wondered what my brother Morris would have done. I knew he wouldn't have tapped out.

Dede yelled, “Tap out Dora Winifred!” I got whacked down to the ground so bad, I saw stars. The next hit put me back down while I tried getting back up. The onlookers cheered even louder.

My eyes cracked open to witness Jermaine climbing out of the ditch as the Gammas embraced him. Just as Jermaine tried escaping, I pounced on him like a leopard attaching its prey. I yelled, “It ain’t over nigga,” as I put him in a chokehold and looked at DeDe.

Dede slow clapped and said, “Congrats pledge Dora Winifred Read. Looks like you get to join the winner’s circle and remain a pledge of the Gamma Alpha Gamma fraternity.” Then he gestured towards the other winners, who sat traumatized, bloody, and cold in a camp area through the valley of ditches.

Even though I won the battle, I felt defeated on the walk of shame. Each ditch had someone sleeping in it, including Jameson, the preppy pledger. The frat members started retrieving the damaged bodies from the ditches. Jameson's jaw was broken, and his face was disfigured. Others were still unconscious.

My friend Raphael was the one who beat up Jameson. I chastised him as soon as he started bragging about it. We looked as if we were about to be the next fight until, Dede yelled, "Settle the commotion. How dare you two fight amongst your fellow brothers. Do y'all have any idea how bad that shit looks on me? It shows you lack discipline. It shows you lack heart! What you pledges' need is someone to teach you some discipline."

DeDe balled his hands into fists as the other brothers crowded in. One Gamma handed him a notebook. Then Dede read, "Instill in you the heart that makes you Gammas. Now I am your pledge master, but I can't do all that disciplining and instilling. So, I am going to assign each one of you a big brother. Your big brother will have the ability to do as he pleases with you. All the tasks your big brother assigns you are only an addition to what I assign you, not a replacement. From now on, you will refer to your big brother as daddy. You will refer to me as daddy. You will only call your pledge brothers by their pledge names. Am I understood?"

Everyone except for me said, "Yes sir!"

Dede shouted back, "See, y'all already aren't listening!" Then gammas crowded us with paddles and belts. Dede continued, "Let's try that again! Am I understood?"

This time he identified my reluctance. Once Dede realized I wasn't submitting, he sicked the Gammas on me and my line brothers. After they physically got their point across, Dede condescendingly said, "Look what you did to your brothers." When I didn't take accountability for that, he sicked them on us again.

This time they stripped me of my will. I was already exhausted from going to war with Jermaine. Now, I was beaten down even worse and couldn't even fight back. Saying, "Yes daddy," hurt me to my soul. My pride is my word. They say pride will get you killed, but I couldn't let my pledge brothers get killed over my pride.

DeDe told us to meet back at 6:00 AM the next morning and advised us to appoint a leader. If we didn't have one selected by the next morning, we would be subject to beatings again. My line brothers and I debated on how the leader should be and to my surprise, they didn't suggest me. They judged my pride and saw it as a flaw. I didn't think they had enough pride, so we were all at odds. Ever since Morris disappeared, all I wanted was brotherhood and it didn't appear I could get the type of brotherhood I wanted from the Gamma fraternity. I didn't have any support from my line brother, so I had to go to the source I could get it from.

Chapter 5: Louisiana

It felt like I washed all the horror away after showering. I had to get my freshest after experiencing such a filthy night. Nakia greeted me with the warmest smile when I exited her bathroom. She had been wanting to take me to the Louisiana Catfish Festival, but I had no clue it would be under these circumstances.

Nakia thought I was overdressed, but I could tell she was proud to have me by her side. Louisiana seemed to have popping parties non-stop. A band that sounded good enough to play at the Super Bowl was the entertainment at the fest. The guitar strings, keyboard jingles, and accordion made me feel like a local. The smell of fried catfish reminded me of what I was there for.

Nakia reminded me that I was there for something else when she interrupted my meal by asking me to dance. I forgot about everything that happened the previous night and everyone around us while we grooved as if it was just us on the dancefloor. I snapped out of the magical trance when she called me brother while we were talking in between songs.

Her calling me brother felt like she was falsely friend-zoning me. Nonetheless, her sending me mixed signals was the least of my concerns when another man got her attention. She asked me to wait a minute, then hurried off with her head down and without telling me who she was going to talk to.

I watched as she approached a guy wearing a black leather jacket, sunglasses, and an afro. Look like he just transported from a 1970s disco ball. I wondered what I should do while their conversation heated up. Nakia seemed to have a lot of intense conversations everywhere she went. Their conversation ended with an exchange of money and an envelope.

She hurried in my direction, then said, "Let's talk my brother," as she guided me back to our table. Nakia deflected my questions to question me about last night. When I played that same game with her she said, "I heard you had trouble taking orders." I snapped back, "What? Your boyfriend is running his mouth about me huh?"

She took a deep breath and said, "Not exactly. We had a fight yesterday, and he reached out to apologize. We ended up talking about your whole pledging routine."

When I asked Nakia is that why she asked me here, I was slightly relieved she asked am I still having trauma with Morris's disappearance. She read me like a book and got straight to the point. That's what I loved about her.

I looked away and answered, "All the time. I just miss him so much Nakia. He was more than a brother to me. He was a part of me. Sinclair brought him up to me the other day and I flashed out on him. Life can't go on the same without him."

Nakia interjected, "That's why you need to pursue the case."

I took my anger out on her and said, "Nakia, how many times I gotta tell you. There ain't no case. He's gone for good."

When she realized she wasn't getting through to me she presented some articles about the KKK kidnappings in the 1980s, but I wasn't trying to hear it. I didn't believe that was my brother's fate. Dustin began blowing up my phone, but I didn't answer. I expressed to her my disappointment about them not selecting me as the leader. She responded, "If you want to be a leader of a black fraternity you need to get involved in black issues. Not only that, you need to get more organized. You can start by coming to Senator Avery's rally for the support of Terrence Grey's family."

I told her I wasn't getting involved in politics and she defensively responded, "This isn't politics my brother. This is our lives. Senator Avery is the first Louisiana Senator to unapologetically bring attention to the black community in this magnitude. A white man with true love for our culture. The kinds of laws he wants to pass will expose and extinguish the institutions that allow brothers like Morris to get kidnapped by white supremacists every day!" Once I shook my head, she abruptly stood up and said, "I have black people to help. Maybe when you stop living in fantasy land, you can join me." Then stormed off.

(Part 2 Update)

“Uh 1, 2, and uh 3,” said the new brotha on stage before the band behind him hit the drums.

The music turned back to a Cajun vibe as I watched Nakia brush past Dustin, making his untimely appearance as usual.

“Damn, what’s her deal D Dub?” Dustin asked.

I took a deep breath and responded, "You know how heated she gets when discussing politics. Listen, Dustin, I was out of line last night. I should've been thinking about y'all and not just…"

He looked at the two girls he was dancing with, then said, "Let me stop you there! This ain't the time, brother." Then introduced me to Maggie and Jessica. Jessica stopped dancing with them and approached me with lust in her eyes. Everyone appeared to be down for a fun night, so we went on an adventure.

Chapter 6: Barbie Girl

Maggie jumped in the back of Jessica's whip with Dustin as we left the Catfish festival for the Gamma crib. Jessica had a pink convertible Mercedes with black leather seats. Her Barbie doll looks matched her entire swag. I jokingly called her Barbie Girl, and the name stuck.

I didn't realize how smitten I was until I gave her my government name, and Dustin called me out on it. When she assured me that she liked my name, I knew I was in.

Dustin suggested that Jess should take the scenic route so he and Maggie could get to know each other better. Jess rubbed my left forearm and said, "I want to get to know Dagobert better too. He's a cutie. Oh my gosh, Maggie, isn't he?"

"Alright, alright," Dustin said before Maggie could answer. "We busy back here."

Once Jessica turned onto a dimly lit street, she said, "I know who you are Dagobert. Why did you quit the football team? You look like you can still play."

When I denied telling her the real reason, and she persisted, I realized she was on a mission. She acted as if she wanted to learn everything about me in one night. Once I realized the questions weren't about to slow up, I asked, "What do you want to know?"

She took the lead as the aggressor and answered, "Enough to get you out on a date. Enough to get to know what you're all about. I want to learn what your interests are and who you are." When I took a moment to respond, she added, "I know that's a lot for a passenger, princess."

I rubbed her hand and said, "I'm more of a passenger King, but I want to get to know you too."

Jessica blushed and responded, "You are quite a smooth gentleman. I have to watch you! Okay, Dagobert. I'm a pre-law student for starters. I study poli sci and I like to write, but that's all you get for now. At least until we have a part two to this date."

I interjected, "Oh, is this a date now? I have never been a double date kind of dude. We need to pick a place for our romantic first date. I know a couple of spots in town. Ima just need your number." She gave it to me as soon as we arrived at fraternity row. I knew Dustin and I had other things to do, but I didn't want to part ways with her.

The Gammas lived on the tallest hill in town. It always took us time and sweat to get up there. We were back at the big crib at 5:30 sharp. The whole pledge class pulled up early. I saw Raphael bark as he organized the others. He really thought he was the leader.

"Alright y'all. Let's get it!" he lectured us.

Before he could say another word, a tomato blasted him in the face.

Raphael yelled, "What the hell! Who did that?"

Once my line brothers and I started laughing, people began pegging us with tomatoes. All of our outfits were ruined while we tried to protect ourselves. When the tomatoes stopped, DeDe yelled through a megaphone from the front balcony, saying, "Good evening worms, report to the great room immediately!"

We dragged our sorry behinds through the front door, defeated and embarrassed. I wondered, "Is this all pledging is? Getting humiliated repeatedly. Getting your butt whooped repeatedly." I thought pledging was about leadership and brotherhood. So far, it's been all about this bull jive.

Without the party going on, I noticed all the artwork: portraits of alumni on the walls, composites hung with golden frames, chandeliers draped over us from the height of a two-floor ceiling, and they were colored with the Gamma gold, green, and purple colors.

DeDe continued, “Congratulations! You made it this far. Now, who is your leader?” When no one responded, he asked, “Have you not picked?”

I put my brothers before me for the first time in this pledge process. "We nominate Raphael," I said.

DeDe asked, "Are you going to step up, Raphael?"

He was caught off guard, but stepped up and answered, “Yes.”

DeDe affirmed him by saying, "Good choice, gentlemen. Get to the front of the line, Raphael." Raphael timidly walked to the front with no confidence. DeDe continued, "Now, let's see if y'all can make it past phase 2. I'm going to get things ready for y'all. In the meantime, these fine brothers are going to show you a good time. Take it away, Q."

He stepped forward and said, "Alright, you little punks. Single file line. Down the basement now!"

Q and a few other frat leaders guided us down a flight of stairs. We inched slowly to a door at the bottom. Q yelled at Raphael to open the door.

Raphael opened the door and walked into a pitch-black room. Q yelled again and said, "Get the hell down! Cue the music!" Then he slammed the door.

We all got to our knees.

Then a kid's song lyrics started playing,

"Hiya Barbie!"

"Hi, Ken!"

"You wanna go for a ride?"

"Sure, Ken!"

"Jump in!"

"I'm a Barbie girl in the Barbie world. Life in plastic, it's fantastic! You can brush my hair, undress me everywhere. Imagination, life is your creation."

"Come on, Barbie, let's go party!" The beat raced, and the lyrics repeated.

Q yelled, "Sing along, pledges!"

"I'm a Barbie girl in the Barbie world," we all start singing in unison.

"Clap your hands above your heads as you sing!" Q yelled again as we followed his command.

"Uh, uh, uh yeah," we sang as our hands smacked against each other. "Come on barbie, let's go barbie. Ooh ooh, ooh , ooh."

Singing Barbie Girl in this pitch-black room while clapping my hands over my head was about the dumbest thing I've ever done. As dumb as this crap was, at least I wasn't getting my butt whooped.

We continued singing and clapping before I noticed the number of voices decreasing. Pledges were being snatched one by one. Before long, it was just Dustin and me singing. I could tell it was Dustin; he sang like a Barbie girl.

When they snatched Dustin, my heart dropped. I kept singing and clapping all by myself in the dark room. I couldn't see a thing. Now, I was scared.

"Come on, Barbie, let's go, barbie," I sang before being snatched up by several gammas who put a bag over my head. I couldn't breathe or see, and my feet were lifted off the ground until they planted me in a chair. Then DeDe asked, "Are you ready to die nigga?"

Chapter 7: Big Brother

I gasped for air. When they pulled my mask off, I saw DeDe standing over me. The prez, Antoine, stood beside him. All the brothers were dressed in black hoodies with the Gamma letters across the chest.

"Where are my pledge brothers?" I asked.

DeDe said, "Don't worry about them. They already got their business taken care of. Now, it's time for us to take care of you. Pledge Dora Winifred Read, are you ready for the next phase of your Gamma pledge period? Do you think you man enough?"

Morris taught me how to be a man. My pops was around for my childhood, but not when I had to grow up. The only male figure I had to look up to was Morris.

Sinclair looked up to my mom. He was never truly raised to be a man. As I reflected, I realized Nakia was right. It doesn't matter what our differences are. I should've been that man for Sinclair. I still need to be.

I proudly said, "I am man enough!"

I looked confident on the surface, but inside, I was shaking. It's not in my nature to show fear, but that's how Morris molded me.

DeDe and Antoine moved aside to display the one thing that could make this crap worse. Right in front of me, I saw Apollo - the short, dark-skinned brotha with hazel eyes and a brand running from his neck to shoulders.

Antione said, "Pledge Dora Winifred Read, honor is among the most important Gamma Brother traits. Virtue is another. Plus, intelligence and strength, but the trait that all Gamma Brothers must possess above all – brotherhood."

Apollo handed me a folded purple hoodie. The other brothers cut my hands free, and I grabbed it. I spread it out in front of me, raising it with awe. Letters! My first letters! Antione said, “Now, you are officially a Neophyte of the Gamma Alpha Gamma Fraternity. Meet your big brother.”

I move the hoodie aside to see that little dark-skinned meatball whose girl I hooked up with last night.

Apollo said, "Welcome to the fam, little bro."

Apollo dapped me up and pulled me from the chair. All the brothers went crazy and started popping champagne bottles. My whole pledge class reappeared wearing the same Neophyte purple hoodie. I saw everybody's big brother. Dustin was assigned Q, and Raphael was assigned DeDe. They looked just alike anyway.

Dede addressed my pledge class and said, "Y'all listen up. Your big brother is your role model and friend, but they have a weight much heavier than that. If you mess up, only your big brother has the power to expel you. If I want to expel you for any reason, your big brother must agree first. With that being said, it is in your best interest to keep your big brother as happy as possible."

Antione said, "This night marks something great in each and every one of your lives. Each Gamma family is predicated on uplifting the black community. Our community. Y'all are about to learn what brotherhood is all about. Get your little brother ready and introduce them to your family."

Apollo nudged me and said, "Come on homie. I want to show you something."

He ignored my questions as we walked through the gamma backyard and dopest basketball court on this side of the Mississippi river. There was a hot tub and swimming pool, vehicles I could never hope to afford, and a little barbecue spot that sat on a brick penthouse.

Apollo's green Raptor truck sat at the crown of the lot, overlooking the other whips. "How do y'all afford all this?" I asked as he reached for his keys.

He responded, "Man, the Gammas have a strong Alumni base, and they donate to us all the time. In return, they expect us to achieve academically and put in work for the black community."

I interjected, "I ain't know y'all were involved in the community like that."

He sighed and said, "Yeah, we kind of fell off. We used to be heavily involved in that regard. We did our thing in those good ol' days when my big brother was president."

"Your big bro was president? Who was that?" I asked.

When he told me about his brother, I asked, "Damn, so you got some pull in the frat then?"

He became defensive and said, “Never call it a frat. But, I'm part of the Gamma Beta family homie. That's one of the oldest Gamma families, second only to Gamma Alpha. If you make it past pledging, you will be part of that family someday. That's a huge responsibility, kid."

I hated that he called me kid, but I kept my disapproval to myself. I asked, “Who’s in Gamma Alpha?”

When he told me, Antione, I immediately asked if DeDe was too.

“Antoine is a Gamma Alpha,” he said after I put the window back up.

“What about DeDe?” I inquired.

He sucked his teeth and said, “Hell, how do you think he got the pledge master gig over…” He bit his tongue without pressing his teeth against it, then continued, “They are both Gamma Alpha fam. Their legacy runs deep, too.”

"Families are one thing, but the Gamma brotherhood is concrete. We're all brothers. Anyways, the Gamma Betas have some serious legacy too. You'd be surprised to see some of our alums. We have a legacy of activism. My big brother was in law school. I'm in law school. Maybe you'll get into law school."

I didn't give his suggestion much thought. I was more concerned about our destination. While we walked up to the old house, I noticed gargoyle statues on each side of the door. They were identical statues from the Gamma crib. The Greek letters Gamma Beta were written on the door.

Behind closed doors was a museum filled with historical Gamma members and some of the best art I ever saw. While marveling at the gallery, he said, "During the early 1900s and times of civil unrest, the Gamma families used these hideouts as spots to meet up and mobilize against our enemies. These secret hideouts were safe places for any African American terrorized by racist cops, politicians, and vigilante groups."

Apollo stopped my daydream when he suggested I check out an artifact. I was shocked to my core when I read the name Morris Waller Sr.

I didn't even know my dad attended college. For him to be a Gamma blew my mind. My mom always told us he went straight to the military.

Another surprise was waiting for me when he pointed to the name Morris Waller Jr. engraved in gold. He was honored for being an African American community organizer, political activist, and police accountability student lawyer.

My big brother? A Gamma? What! And here I thought we were so close. I knew Morris like I knew myself, but he hid this from me. I wanted to be mad at him for lying to me, but all I could do was marvel at the type of man he was. Becoming a Gamma was more than letters. Being a gamma was in my bloodline.

Chapter 8: The Senator

You have reached Sinclair Waller. I am busy right now and cannot come to the phone. Please leave your name and number, along with a brief message, and I will get back to you," was the automated message I kept getting when I reached out to my little brother. I stopped my day to call and looked defeated when another call went unanswered.

Nakia spotted me as soon as I picked my head up. She knew more about Gamma than I did. After finding out about my family ties, I changed my wardrobe to show off my Gamma lineage. She noticed it the first time she saw him. After approaching me, she asked, "Who's the Gamma in your family?"

I smirked and responded, "You mean, who are the gammas in my family? My dad and big brother were Gammas."

Her face lit up, and then she insinuated, "Oh, you aren't only in it for the girls anymore?"

Nakia's inquiry seemed like another invitation to get out of the friend zone. Showing up to her favorite politician's event was another attempt to get out of the friend zone. While we grinned at each other, applause and his presence on stage settled the crowd.

Nakia held on to my arm while I pushed through the crowd to get us up front. Once we got there, I had my first in-person look at Senator Aaron Avery. He was a country liberal and former basketball player, quite different from any politician I'd ever seen.

Once the crowd became quiet, he passionately said, "You know, I've been all over the beautiful state of Louisiana. I love this state from the bottom of my heart. My humble hometown of Natchitoches is only 3 hours from this very campus. Like most of you, I had to scratch and claw my way to get to where I am today. I had to fight through some of the ugliest aspects of poverty this country has to offer. But unlike most of you, I had a privilege - white privilege. White privilege is a privilege that can put even the poorest white man miles ahead of any black man in this country. I, myself, am man enough to admit that I benefited from that privilege. As dirt poor as my life was, I knew it was better than that of the blacks in my same situation. As a matter of fact, not only did I benefit from white privilege, but I also made it to the top on the shoulders of the black community. As many of you know, I played basketball at this very university. For several years, I played in the NBA, a majority black fan base. But what you may not know is that I learned the game of basketball from black folks. Growing up, I played against black men who were far better than me. Sure, I had the size and good looks, but I was nothing compared to some of those athletes. But I had more looks at a college scholarship because I was white. All my success in politics stems from my recognition as an athlete. If you ask me today, I owe my life to black people! The least I can do is give them something in return! After decades in politics, I have yet to deliver on my debt to the black community. I ask you now, here, today.... Help me deliver on my debt to the black community! But you know, I'm not the only one who owes a debt to the black community. Black people built this country. The United States rose to power off the backs of enslaved black and brown men, women, and children for 400 years! I'd say there's about 50 states that owe a debt to the black community!"

Then he put the mike down as the crowd erupted. Once they erupted, he continued, "I want to pivot to something near and dear to my heart. And that's the recent cases of police brutality in your community. Our community! Police shootings of black men and women shouldn't just be troubling to the black community. It should be troubling to all Americans. And the recent lynching of Terrence Grey put my soul in a dark place. Notice, I called it a lynching because that's what it was - a public lynching. But to fight police violence, I'm going to need your help. I am asking each of you to scan the barcode on our flyers right now."

As people pulled their phones out, the senator continued, "This barcode will take you to our fundraising website for anti-police violence. I am asking each and every one of you to donate at least ten dollars. This money is going directly to the family of Terrence Grey. Any additional proceeds will be used to fund the Justice and Policing Act we want to implement once we take office. This Act will keep black men and women out of harm's way when it comes to police violence."

The senator proved that I misjudged him. I felt most of his speech. However, my mind was elsewhere. Later that night, I set up a date with Barbie girl and decided to leave the event once Apollo invited me to get crawfish.

Nakia acted as if I didn't even show up for the event when I told her I was leaving. Before I knew it, her and I were fussing like a married couple. Arguing in public brought even more toxicity to the altercation. Our fuss ended after we stormed off in separate directions.

I was seeing red until Apollo texted, "Little bro, are you on the way?"

That reminded me to reach out to Sinclair again. Before I could dial his number, Barbie girl intercepted me. She tried intercepting me from Apollo too. She asked if our date could be moved up a night because she was alone and lonely at home.

Chapter 9: Little Brother

When I arrived at Jessica's place, she greeted me as if I was the man of the lavish house she lived in.

I tried leading her upstairs, but she said, "Wait, I want to get to know you more first. Let me get us some wine."

We had small talk while she was in the kitchen. Her plan to get to know me went out of the window when she returned with the wine. After setting the bottles down, she straddled me and then stuck her tongue in my mouth. She must have already had wine because she knocked her glass of wine over. She panicked and said, "I have to clean this up before-"

An opening door broke her statement. She did her best to play it off and clean up the mess. Once she made the place look somewhat presentable, a familiar face appeared in the kitchen. It was Senator Avery.

Without acknowledging me, he said, "Jessica, you should have been there to see your father!" Someone trailing behind him cut him off. A short woman with a strong southern accent said, "Oh, I didn't know we were having company."

"Neither did I," the politician added.

"Mommy, daddy, this is Dagobert," Barbie girl said.

"Hello, Dagobert. Are you joining us for dinner?" Her mother asked.

Barbie girl looked at me and interjected, "Yes, baby. You are staying."

Jessica volunteered my presence before I could answer. Her calling me baby made things even more awkward.

After Jessica put some more modest clothes on, we all gathered at the dinner table to enjoy some Jambalaya. Me, Barbie-girl, Mrs. Avery, the senator, and Jessica's younger brother Parker, who was a straight-up weirdo. He had long, greasy black hair covering his face and he hunched over to the side of his chair, doodling on a notebook.

"Parker, no drawing at the dinner table," the senator said.

I looked at the woman of the house and said, "This Jambalaya is delicious, Mrs. Avery. And you have a beautiful family. Is this all of you?"

"Not at all Dagobert," the senator answered for his wife. "I have two other boys. Ed plays college basketball in North Carolina. Owen plays defensive tackle in Alabama."

This was wild. I was sitting across from the next senator of Louisiana. Nakia would freak out if she knew.

"You got some athletes on your hands sir," I said as I chewed on a piece of juicy and spicy shrimp.

"Yes, they take after my frame a bit more than the boy over there." He pointed at Parker, who made a disturbed face and looked down at the table. "But if you don't mind me saying, it looks like you're quite the athlete as well, Dagobert. You played for the school football team didn't you?"

I proudly answered, "Yes, I did sir. I played running back, but I ain't never start or nothing".

"Dago is being way too modest, Daddy," Jessica jumped in. "Not only did he play running back, but his brother was drafted to play professionally."

The Senator leaned forward and asked, "You don't say? What team did he play for?"

"Houston," I responded with no enthusiasm.

He smiled and said, "Oh, really? I was a huge Houston fan back in my NBA days. Playing a few years there gave me access to some football games. What is his name?"

"Morris Waller Jr." I struggled to let the words out of my mouth.

"Hmm. Doesn't ring a bell," the Senator responded without making eye contact.

If he had looked at my eyes, he would've seen the pain that came with saying my brother's name around a bunch of white strangers at a table. But talking to this dude, I actually started liking him. He's got charisma to him. I noticed it at the rally, but I assumed it was just a show, like most politicians do. But he was actually for real. He had a way of making me want to talk more and reveal info I didn't normally share with strangers.

"He didn't play very long," I continued after a long pause.

"Oh, why is that?" the senator asked.

"He...." My phone starts buzzing.

I looked down to see a number that made my breath sink. Why was she calling me? She knew better than to call my phone, so I pressed the button at the top right of the phone to silence the call.

"Sorry about that," I said.

"Not a problem, Dagobert. You seem like a nice young man." He pointed to my right shoulder and said, "I noticed that you have the Gamma neophyte letters on. You're pledging Gamma Alpha Gamma?"

I smiled and answered, "Uh, yes sir." I was shocked to see he knew what's up. This man really is a brother at heart.

He said, "A fine fraternity the Gammas are. There is a lot of history between those walls. You'll do well to read up on it. Educate yourself. Learn as much as you can about it. Tell me, have the Gammas been following the campaign at all? Their history was heavy on politics and activism."

I took a deep breath and responded, "Not to my knowledge. I'm trying to change that though. I want to be involved as much as possible. My friend Nakia is very active with your rallies. She'd freak out if she knew I was sitting here with you."

The senator wiped his mouth and said, "Good. You should get involved with her. Raise awareness. I'd love to meet her sometime."

"Aaron has been pushing for so many laws to help your community dear," Mrs. Avery said as she touched her husband's hand.

"Mommy, don't say it like that," Jessica hissed as she rolled her neck. She grabbed my hand and put it into her lap, then continued, "Dago, I'm sorry baby." I guess I was *baby* to her now, and I couldn't even get Nakia to stop referring to me as *brother*.

"Nah, it's fine," I said.

"No, it's not," the senator interrupted. "Nothing is fine about how black and brown people are treated in this country. It's about time this country woke up and took a stand."

The passion of his voice was even stronger than at the rally. This brother might just be it.

"Just today, I received word of another black man slaughtered at the hands of police," he shook his head. "The media hasn't released the news yet, but we're expecting it to break any minute now. A statement will be released tomorrow morning."

"That's terrible," Barbie Girl said.

"Yes. A promising young man too. Not mixed up in any street nonsense or drugs. Very tragic case. I have no idea how this country is going to handle the reaction from this one."

My phone buzzed out of control again. I declined the call, but she called me again and again.

"Do you need to get that Dagobert?" the senator asked.

"Yes, excuse me," I wiped my mouth with a handkerchief as I stepped away.

"I thought I told you to never call me again!" I answered the phone.

When I answered, my mom yelled, "Sinclair! He's dead!"

Chapter 10: No justice, No Peace

I looked across the living room to see the flat screen TV display the breaking news headline, "Medical school black student killed by the hands of the police."

The next several hours felt like a blur because my eyes were flooded with tears, and my heart was filled with rage. No condolences could comfort the pain of losing my little brother to police brutality. I didn't regain my senses until I was on stage leading a protest on my brother's behalf.

I couldn't breathe while I stood on a stage, overlooking thousands of protestors of all ages and races. They stood in solidarity, holding signs, marching, and chanting. All of this should have made me feel better, but it didn't.

While thousands stood before me, only memories of Sinclair replayed in my mind. My little brother never harmed anyone and was an asset to this universe. What hurt even worse was that he died while we were on bad terms, and I never got the opportunity to express how much I loved him. My mind was wrapped around the last conversation we had.

Nakia interrupted a flashback I didn't want to end by kissing me on my cheek and sympathetically caressing my hands. I now understood her desire for activism. She had the crowd ready to risk their freedom and safety to advocate and protest my brother's death.

The streets had been erupting with protests for three straight days. This was so surreal. My pledge class hovered over me for support. Some of the Gamma brothers were protesting in the crowd. I ain't see my big bro, Apollo, but he called me a couple of days ago to give his condolences.

There was no sign of Antoine or DeDe. It was strange that DeDe wasn't here. He allowed the pledges to support me, but I would think he'd be around for Nakia at least.

The chants got heavy on my ears. I started to zone out as the image of baby bro eclipsed my mind. Then, in the back middle of the protestors, I saw the weirdest thing - a dude standing and wearing an orange-horned masquerade mask. He was wearing a heavy black trench coat.

"Man, you see that over there?" I asked Dustin.

"See what bro?" he asked after looking in the crowd.

When I searched for the masked dude, I couldn't find him. The crowd got too wild to spot anything. Suddenly, I found myself getting dragged by the protestors as they swarmed the streets, stampeding through the city. My pledge brothers kept me upright and held my shoulders.

Nakia took a deep breath and spoke through the megaphone, "Brothers and sisters! How much longer do we need to endure this? How many more times do we need to hear about one of our brothers and sisters slaughtered at the hands of the police? Why must it always be us? Why must it always be the black boys and girls who have the most promising futures? Why America? Why do you hate us?"

The protestors echoed her sentiments and chanted, "Why do you hate us? Why do you hate us? Why do you hate us?"

Nakia exited the stage and led the protest down the central business district of New Orleans. I saw white folks watching from the balconies. People closed their shops down as the protests intensified. Hundreds of people joined us. I looked to my side and saw Gammas all over. Brothers and pledges were on the frontlines, and it wasn't just to support me. It was to stand in solidarity as a community.

Then, a powerful scene developed when I saw them. Antoine led a herd of Gamma brothers with DeDe by his side.

"Gammas!" Antoine yelled.

"We want justice!" the brothers yelled after.

"Gammas!"

"Ain't no peace," the Gammas sang.

I thought Nakia was storming the streets with no destination until she led the crowd to a standoff with law enforcement.

"No justice!" she yelled.

"No peace!" the group followed.

They repeated the chants in unison and synchronicity. Nakia had intentions of a peaceful protest, but that plan crumbled when someone pegged an officer in the head with a rock. The welt on his head marked the start of a riot.

Glass bottles, stones, and other objects rained on the police. They retaliated with smoke bombs that snatched the air out of my lungs. The smoke disbursed the crowd. I was in danger of being the second son my mother lost in one week. I had all the reasons in the world to give up during these moments, but everyone's support for Sinclair and me kept me fighting.

My rapport with the Gamma brothers, friends, and Nakia sparked an entire demonstration. Other protesters adopted our energy and rebellious spirits. The revolution was televised. News cameras and helicopters were cautiously surveilling the riot. Buildings were burned, street signs were toppled over, and blood was shed between law enforcement and civilians.

The thrill of the fight rushed through my veins. Protesting for Sinclair made me more passionate than ever. When my sight was clear again, Nakia jumped into my arms. Our passionate adrenaline made our lips magnetic. We kissed in the middle of the protest and shifted the energy in the crowd.

Nakia and I instantly remembered where we were when we heard people cheering. The smile on her face made me realize our interest had been mutual before that moment.

I'd remember this moment forever, along with the next one. The following memory will be one I'll try forgetting for a lifetime.

As soon as Nakia took a few steps in the other direction, a smoke bomb stopped her in her tracks. The thicker layers of smoke blinded me from everyone except for a masked man pointing a gun at me.

Chapter 11: The Organization

Dreaming about Sinclair distorted my reality when I regained consciousness. Someone with an unfamiliar accent woke me up and said, "Good morning my darling. I am the doctor who will be completing your testing. I asked them for one like you, and they did not disappoint."

Suddenly, I hear doors slide open with a jingle like an elevator alarm. "What are you doing doctor?"

A dark voice asked. The Doctor responded, "The experiment."

I could barely distinguish what they looked like, but they all had long white capes and masks.

The leader walked to the side of my test tube and asked, "How much longer?"

The Doctor dropped his head and responded, "I would like a few more days. He is a fit specimen, so he would probably survive the testing."

"Have you gathered the data you needed?" The leader interrupted.

The Doctor pleaded, "Yes, I have. But I need a few more days to..."

Kablam!! The masked leader punched through my glass tube. The fluid poured out. I felt my body drain like I was being whirlpooled down the suction of a toilet as it flushed.

I fell to the ground as the chemical covered the floor around me before sinking into the containment mats. My body burned, and my neck felt like a ringed towel.

The leader condescendingly said, "Look at this. He is pathetic and begging for help. Give him a hand."

Other members of the vigilante group lifted me up. I hung from their shoulders, unable to feel my legs.

He continued, "See, we lift you up. It's just like your kind to ask for a handout. Well, here's a handout." The handout he was referring to smacked me in the face. Once my face went numb, he yelled, "You baboon looking Ape."

"Stop it! You're ruining his flesh!" the European Doctor yelled.

The leader shouted back, "His flesh is already ruined. He is a nigger doctor! We break them down so you can build them up, Doctor!" Then, he broke my arm as if he were dismembering a chicken wing.

While I anguished in pain, he raised his voice to drown out my cries and yelled, "He will learn soon enough. Doctor, see to it that this boy gets through all your testing procedures. My men went through a lot of trouble to get their hands on a nigger like this. We will terminate you if you cannot maximize your results with this one. Understood?"

The Doctor showed his submissiveness when he silently nodded. When the leader and his gang left, the Doctor led me to a radiation chamber, then scurried off like a rodent.

Once I was locked in, the Doctor spoke through the intercom, "Welcome to your new home, my darling! You will live in this room for the next week or so!"

Chapter 12: Pain

I spoke to my little brother's spirit, "Sinclair, why was I not there for you? Even hearing you speak of your medical stories for hours is missed in my heart. You were my guy for real, but I was not the man I should have been for you. I thought I was a man because of how Morris raised me and all of the girls I got. I had it all wrong."

The self-reflection hurt worse. I reflected, "I ain't no man at all, and now he's gone. I'm sitting here in this radiation chamber, suffering through excruciating pain."

It had been five days, and my lungs collapsed. I could hear my damn heartbeat. Something was taking control of me. My skin was peeling like I was a snake, and my lips were crusty, stinging with pain. Fifteen pounds of muscle was gone just that quick. I felt that this was my punishment for how I treated Sinclair.

I've thought about taking my own life, but I was too weak and had no methods of killing myself. All I could do was soak in my own pity.

Two other black men were brought in. One died within a matter of minutes. The other one was named Bobby. He looked like he would be next to die. Bobby asked me, "When do you think we're getting out of here?"

I had no room for optimism or strength to answer. He continued, "I think a miracle will save us." I pleaded for him to kill me, but he didn't have the strength to do it either. Neither was he in the proximity.

The Doctor came in every day to feed us and give us IVs. I think it was his efforts that kept us alive. I knew the leader wanted us dead and tortured. When I thought the Doctor was entering the room again, I had his identity mistaken. An obese person in a radiation suit hurried to my chamber and dragged me out. I asked a question I instantly regretted asking. The suspicious guy whispered the Doctor is dead.

Bobby's prediction was right, but he didn't benefit from it. I asked the suspicious guy about saving Bobby, and he responded, "He's too big and good as dead. I don't have enough time to save the both of you. The Dragons will be here any minute once they hear the Doctor is unresponsive. We got to go ASAP."

The suspicious guy with an innocent look on his face named Rocky put me on his shoulders and carried me to an escape route in the ceiling. I wanted to scream out free at last but could only yell in anguish as the sun baked my skin.

Steam sizzled from my burning skin. Once my skin settled, I looked up to the sight of black German Shepherds and a fenced backyard. Rocky grinned and devilishly said, "You thought I was going to save you nigger? Dogs, sick 'em!"

The biggest hound charged at me first, tackling me on my back before it dug its sharp razor blade teeth into my broken arm. The other two went for my legs, and the animals ripped into me. They shred my peeling skin apart and pound their snouts into my flesh like hyenas scavenging on a buffalo carcass.

Rocky's innocent look faded while he trolled me and scooped a handful of chewing tobacco. I never thought I would have wanted to hear the Doctor's voice until he yelled, "You fool! What are you doing? You could have killed him!"

Rocky was a master manipulator. He put an innocent look back on his face and said, "Hey, the captain told me to make sure the experiment can handle all the pain we bring him."

While they fussed and put me back in the chamber, I realized Bobby's lifeless body. I only had a few brief interactions with him, but his death saddened me. In a defeated voice, I pleaded for them to kill me next.

The Doctor coddled me and responded, "I need you alive. You are a survivor. Now keep surviving." Then, he proceeded to stick a needle in my neck to draw blood. Once the blood was drawn, it was poured into a test tube and continued, "Perfect. Your body is ready for the first fungi release. We will begin the next phase of experimentation now."

I regretted not paying attention to Sinclair's medical and scientific talk when the Doctor started talking medically and scientifically.

Rocky added, “You better hope for your sake that this crap works doc. Our fraternity is close-knit, and for us to trust an outsider like you with this, it better pay off."

"Trust me, you will have nothing but good news to report to your superiors," the Doctor said as Rocky brought me back to the laboratory chair.

After an undetectable amount of time went by, the Doctor said, "Congratulations, my darling. You now weigh 143 pounds, 100 less than when you started. You have survived the first phase of your testing. Only one other man has made it this far. Now, the easy part."

A sunbed cover closed above me. Bright lights flashed on, and the Doctor's voice came through a speaker. "Brace yourself my dear. You are about to make history."

Gas flooded the sunbed. Once the whole tube was filled with gas, a warm liquid began displacing it. I felt it cover my ears as I sunk into it. Then, needles appeared. They pierce through my limbs, and I spazzed around like I was having a seizure. I felt the injections throughout my body and fungi pumping through my veins.

Chapter 13: Gamma

Rocky's fist crashed into my cheek, throwing me against the wall. I helplessly slid to the floor. "Fight back!" he yelled.

"It will take some time," the Doctor added.

Rocky yelled, "We ain't got time doc! It's already been a month, and he needs to be ready in time for the White Dance." Then he stormed out.

The Doctor turned to me and said, "I do apologize my darling. The people in this organization are not a reflection of me."

Rocky returned moments later with the leader and the other members of the vigilante group.

When they reappeared, the Doctor pierced my neck with a foot-long needle and injected me with something. Then he stepped back, examined my eyes, shined his flashlight in my mouth, and exclaimed, "Success! The specimen's body is a cladosporium sphaerosperum habitat at this point. I have traced the level of radiation to well above expected. I have just injected him with the last family of fungi. It will take some time for them to adjust to their new habitat."

The leader's excitement did not match the Doctor's excitement. He yelled, "You just told me that this operation was a success! You are requesting time that you no longer have, Doctor! We need this boy ready and presentable for the White Dance!"

The Doctor begged for time and asked for him to reschedule the event. The leader raised his voice even louder and screamed, "That is not an option, Doctor! I've been told you to run the Gamma test! The White Dragon rituals are set for specific times, per tradition. Tradition that is not to be tampered with. The event must be up to standard for the Grand Dragon!"

I saw the pink color leave Rocky's ghostly face. His jaw dropped as horror came over it. "The... the Grand Dragon will be at the White Dance?" he asked.

"Yes, and I will be sure to inform him about your lack of seriousness when it comes to masking yourself." The captain pointed into Rocky's chest as the big man shrank with fear. "He will not be pleased to learn you have been showing your face around in front of the doctor and experiment. Nor will he be pleased with me, if I do not deliver the black boy on time. The Grand Dragon is a busy man, and he will take it as a personal sign of disrespect if anything is short of perfection for his visit."

He turned from Rocky and shoved a pistol into the doctor's stomach. "Now, doctor. The Gamma test. I won't ask again."

The Doctor frantically unstrapped me, and Rocky dragged me to another testing area. The Doctor fingered through some buttons and pulled different levers. The platform started shaking like an earthquake. The suspense built up as the roaring sound of the machine powering up damaged my eardrums.

My body expanded and contracted. The Gamma radiation fueled my bloodstream. After a deafening boom, I blacked out into white space.

Chapter 14: The White Dance

When I regained consciousness, I wished to return to the darkness. I woke up chained down in the back of a sketchy van, dressed in a black latex suit. I felt to the point of no return after looking at my reflection. Dagobert Waller and Dora Winifred Read did not exist anymore.

My heart dropped when the van slammed on its brakes. After getting dragged out of the car, Rocky put a bag over my head and tied a rope around my neck. Several hands raised me to my feet. Then, someone jammed a shotgun against my lower back and pushed me forward.

After a half-mile of walking, I was forced into a small boat.

We weren't on the boat for long. After being forced back on land and guided by a shotgun, we began walking a swampy trail. My feet got heavier with every step.

"Stop! Unmask the thing!" The leader yelled.

Before me stood a sea of enraged men shouting slurs in my direction. They were all facing me and paving a pathway in between them for passage. They were touting torches and flags on each side. The banners were white with an orange outline of a dragon's head. The Greek letters 'Alpha Phi' were on each side of its head. The words beneath read "ανώτερη φυλή."

Once I settled in the middle, the captain yelled, "Go!" My resistance made them carry me to the end of the path. A giant, twice the size of the world's largest man, awaited me. The closer I stepped to him, the smaller I became. The giant was dressed differently from the rest. He wore a robe like the Klan, covering his whole body and face with a pointed cap hooding his head. His robe was a crisp orange with black markings on it. He lounged like an orangutan with his long arms spread so wide that his wingspan covered the whole front stage.

On each side of him, there were five men dressed in white robes that looked like his. To the right of him, sat a massive crate. This organization was a next-level vigilante group. They were a secret society within society. White Dragon members disguised their voices and appearances so they could blend right into society.

When I got within 20 feet, he pulled a lever that lifted the crate. It was another black man in the bare, stripped of his muscle and physique. He was curled up like an embryo. Also, he had lesions all over his skin like me. Those weren't our only similarities.

Tears flooded my eyes, and then I yelled, "Morris! Morris! Morris!" He began crying on sight also once we locked eyes. We both were struck down by our oppressors after reuniting.

"Grand Dragon, we are honored to have you here," the captain said as he kneeled while Rocky secured me.

"Morris!" I screamed as I watched him curled by the gigantic Grand Dragon like a house pet. Suddenly, my hands heated. I looked down and saw purple sparks glistening from my fingertips.

Morris somehow found the will to stand while everyone was focused on me. He pointed in my direction, then a beam of purple energy jolted to my chest. The army of White Dragon men tried to stop him. The captain and Rocky grabbed me, but the rays torched my skin, burning through their metal gloves.

In seconds, my body burned, and purple sparks flew from my skin. My arms and legs started glowing.

I stared at Morris as he cried, and his face folded like a handkerchief. The White Dragon men piled on top of him. “Morris!” I yelled before the purple jolt of energy overloaded me, and I watched my body detonate like a bomb.

Chapter 15: Coming Home

I blasted through a ceiling and crashed through a rock-hard surface into water. My lungs were crushed from the impact, and my eyes were shut. I felt my life escaping me as I began sinking in the water. I knew what I needed to do to survive, but I couldn't force my body to do it.

I wanted nothing more than to die, but that was before I saw Morris. Now, I needed to find the will to live. My eyes popped open. Then, I thrust my arms back and threw my body out of the water like a dolphin at the center of the ocean. I screamed like a madman as I forced myself to the shallow end.

"Dawg, what the hell?" a voice asked.

I looked down as my body throbbed up and down with heavy breaths. In front of me stood a little guy with pierced ears sitting with a beautiful woman. He shouted, "You're Dago!" Then he ran off, dragging his date with him. I had an out-of-body experience when I realized I was back at the Gamma's house.

I quickly pulled myself out of the water and grabbed the closest towel to cover my naked body. Before fully covering myself, I was reduced to tears. I didn't know what was reality and what was a dream.

Anything else I endured could've been explained by a crazy drug trip, but seeing Morris wasn't. He was alive, and I needed to find him. I pushed myself through the pool house and dragged my shivering body across the brick floor.

A familiar voice called my name. Dustin and I locked eyes longer than ever when we spotted each other. He rushed to me, tucked my head into his chest, and gripped my shoulders. After embracing me, he said, "What happened to you man? We thought you ran off."

Instead of responding to his question, I called out for Morris. When I started panicking, Dustin rushed me to a bedroom in the fraternity house. After placing me on a bed, he called out for help.

I couldn't tell who was in the room. I just saw bodies running around as I shivered in bed. I felt people fingering through my mouth, forcing pills and water down. They rushed for bags of ice and laid them on my body beneath the covers. "He's hot as hell!" Dustin yelled. I felt a damp, wet towel placed against my forehead.

I slowly started to settle down after being force-fed water. I felt like they caught me right before death. They slowly nursed me to health. I finally recognized them now. I was surrounded and supported by my line brothers. My non-biological brothers were now stronger, wiser, and more stylish. All of them show me how they were initiated. Once I gathered enough strength to speak, I said, "I really appreciate y'all! How long has it been?"

Everyone's demeanor changed after I asked them that question. Dustin responded, "Hell man, forever. We thought you were never coming back. Yesterday was the first anniversary since you went missing." My line brothers were happy to have me back, but their energy toward me wasn't the same.

Dustin said, "Fam, as much as I missed you, this is the last place you should have come. I prayed every night that you would return. I'm thrilled you're back, but you ain't welcome back with the Gammas."

Chapter 16: Expelled

I walked through the entrance of the Gamma Great room in Dustin's dusty old hoodie and sweatpants, backed by my pledge brothers. As soon as I stepped into the room, I heard the roars of boos from the Gammas. They threw up their middle fingers and cussed me out.

The sight reminded me of the White Dance, but now, it's my own people. People who were once my brothers. I saw the hatred in their eyes and heard the hatred in their words. Toward the front, Antoine and DeDe stood with disappointment written across their faces. As I walked toward them, my pledge brothers abandoned me one by one. Dustin was the last one standing with me.

Once I reached the front, I saw Raphael posted up by DeDe. The look on their faces told me all I needed to know. "You got some nerve coming back here," DeDe hissed as he cracked his knuckles.

Antione said, “Relax DeDe.” DeDe obeyed his order physically but not verbally. He blurted out, you must have been smoking crack. I would have never guessed that Dora Winifred Read would become a crackhead. Why did you come back?”

I humbled myself and responded, “Because I need my fraternity’s help.”

Antione responded, “Well, that’s for damn certain. Just look at you. Looks like the streets got the best of you.” The crowd’s meanmugs turned into laughs.

I pled, “Man, I don’t know what this is all about, but I ain’t run away. I got kidnapped!” I look around the room, begging the brothers, “Y’all got to believe me!”

Antione waved his hand at me as if he were rude to a handler and said, "Man, no one in this room believes a thing you say, Dagobert. You lost all privileges to the benefit of the doubt."

DeDe pointed at me with four fingers bonded together and said, “If you weren’t a liar, we wouldn’t have had to expel you. You would still be pledging Gamma and initiated as a brother, but we ain’t into telling stories like you.”

When they told me I was expelled, I discovered a newfound energy. I cried out, "I thought I couldn't be expelled without my big brother's approval."

Apollo made himself seen and said, "Months ago, I gave them my approval to expel you. I can't believe you're going to stand here and lie to everyone. I'll let you in on a little secret." He tilted his head against my neck and whispered in my ear, "Everyone already knows the truth. So, you might as well fess up to it now."

DeDe asked, "Are you still trying to lie negro? Let me help you out, Dagonerd. You crept behind your big brother's back and tried getting at his girl."

Then all the Gammas booed me. Apollo remorsefully said, "You messed with Diamond! You knew I loved her! After everything I did for you!"

I didn't know what to say. I stood there with my mouth open. The Gamma brothers thought I was less than dirt now. There wasn't anything I could say to change that. I said, "I'm sorry. I'm a different man now."

DeDe blurted out, "Nah, you ain't no man at all! Not then, not now! If you showed up a few months ago, I would've put that iron on you, but you ain't even worth it now."

"Get out! Before I beat you down," Antoine yelled.

When Dustin sided with them, I knew I had been exiled.

I yelled, "Y'all! I promise I got kidnapped! They even kidnapped Morris too!"

"Are you really going to this length?" Antoine asked. I looked around and saw Dustin shaking his head. The stares were more out of pity and disappointment than rage. They made me feel even more pathetic. Antione continued, "I knew you weren't man enough to respect your fraternity big brother, but to see you beg and lie like this is something. Now, I know you ain't even man enough to respect the memory of your bloodline. Your real big brother."

DeDe yelled, "Get out!"

Dustin added, "Please!"

When I didn't comply, several of them started chasing after me. They ran me out of the house and into the streets. Everything I ran and walked past looked unfamiliar until I made it downtown. My soul led me to Nakia. I was running in her direction before I knew where I was headed. When I made it to her place, it was no longer there. The lot that used to have a three-story building was now vacant.

I yelled to the top of my lungs while I felt tears brewing in the back of my eyes. Nearly getting hit by a car stopped me from crying and giving up. "Hey! You need to watch where you're going!" A feminine voice yelled. Her yell was so soft that I didn't take it seriously initially. My vision was blurry, but it became concise when I heard Barbie yelling my name. She stopped traffic to console me. Curse words and horns drowned out her caring words.

Her guiding me to her passenger seat was the last thing I remember before waking up at her place. She had moved forward in life also. Barbie no longer lived with her dad and had a high-rise studio apartment downtown. Many things had to occur in her life to move out of her parents' mansion. She didn't plan on moving out until she finished college.

My spirits were lifted after taking a nap. Barbie purchased me several outfits. The excitement for the new clothes was dulled when I realized my clothes were a few sizes smaller than they used to be. My longing for happiness disappeared when Barbie began questioning why I had ghosted her for a year. Her response was the same as the Gammas when I began telling her my story - she didn't believe me either.

After repeating it three times to show her there were no gaps in my story, she said, “I know you needed some time to heal and space after Sinclair’s death, but I am here for you, and you can tell me the truth about anything, even if it hurts my feelings.”

While she caressed my face and nursed me back to health, I felt conflicted about telling her my suppressed thoughts. After staring into each other's eyes, I said, "I need to find Nakia."

Chapter 17: Homecoming

Confetti rained through the football stadium as our team prepared to square off with the rival Texas squad. Cheerleaders jumped and danced, and the bands competed and drew more attention than the football game. Cookouts on the yard had the football stadium smelling like a smokehouse. The culture was second to none. Homecoming was in the air.

Jessica was the homecoming queen. I was her date, but I was dressed opposite of her. She was elegant, and I was dressed like an undercover cop trying to keep a low profile. I wasn't ready for anyone else to lay eyes on me yet aside from Nakia, and I wanted to support Barbie for homecoming.

While walking to the bathroom, Dustin and I crossed paths. He could barely look me in the eyes. I was proud of his accomplishments, but our bond was no longer the same after he turned his back on me. He coldly greeted me after I warmly embraced him. We didn't even get as far as small talk before the Gammas walked upon us. They approached like a pack of wolves, and I was the prey. Dustin and I walked off to avoid further conflict.

I was happy to make it back to my seat for halftime. Once I was seated, someone on the microphone said, "Next, we have a speech from Nakia Taylor on the importance of advocacy, truth, and justice."

I was enamored by her before she said a word. Nakia was more captivating than I remembered. I never had eyes for Barbie like I had them for Nakia. Her words moved the crowd and garnered many positive reactions, but I didn't hear a word she said because I was too distracted by her beauty, passion, and essence. Once she began wrapping up her speech, I began making my way toward her.

My anxiety began boiling over until we crossed paths near the concession stands. I tried shouting her name, but it came out like a last gasp. She looked at me from head to toe and asked, "And, who might you be, my brother?" My heart hit the ground, and my pride shattered when she looked me in the eyes and didn't remember me.

I pled, "It's me - Dagobert."

She pulled my hood back and said, "Ain't no way! Dagobert Dagobert? This has to be a clone. A skinny clone." Reality sat in when we locked eyes again. She continued, "Wow, it really is you. I thought you were never coming back."

I knew my words and energy were limited, so I got straight to the point and said, "I saw Morris!" Nakia was the last person I thought wouldn't believe my story, but here she was, questioning me like everyone else. I was tired of explaining myself to people.

She drew everyone's attention when she shouted, "You're a liar Dagobert! You don't care about your own people! Why should I believe you about anything after what you did to Apollo? And what you did to your brothers and me! You abandoned me!"

When I reached for her hand, she jerked away from me. A voice interrupted our altercation and yelled, "Get your hand off of my girl, you creep!"

DeDe had his fist balled while Raphael and Apollo stood by his side. Nakia interrupted him and said, "I'm not your girl anymore!"

He responded, "You ain't thinking straight. You don't know what's good for you!" Then DeDe looked at me and said, "You see you! I'm about to lay hands on you."

Apollo interjected, "I have something better for him." Then pulled out a knife.

Raphael backed up, but DeDe and Apollo moved forward.

"Stop this! All of you!" Nakia yelled.

Before being stripped of my strength, I would have easily manhandled them, but that athleticism was long gone. I was frail for the first time in my life.

DeDe charged at me and tackled me into the street. Apollo started kicking me, and DeDe started punching me. I was getting jumped and recorded. My own people did me like the opposition did me.

They began questioning Dustin's loyalty when he tried pulling them off me. "This isn't the way!" Dustin shouted.

Once they were off me, I saw a teenager with an orange mask waving at me. Then, I noticed a red light blinking on the crown of his mask. "Get down!" I screamed. After my scream of caution, an explosion knocked everyone to the ground and sent orange smoke into the atmosphere.

When the smoke cleared, the vigilante group I warned everyone about reappeared. A group of them surrounded us, and everyone looked at me. They regretted not believing me.

One of the White Dragon men forced DeDe on his knees with a dagger pointed at our former pledge master's neck, then said, "You didn't think you would get away from us so easily, did you boy? How about we lynch him in the street?" The goon ripped into his hostage's chin before his blade carved through DeDe's neck in front of us.

"DeDe!" Nakia screamed.

"Big bro!" Raphael yelled from behind Dustin.

I watched in horror as DeDe's limp body fell to the ground. Then, each vigilante member pulled out a weapon.

"Run!" I yelled, pulling Nakia and cutting through the street. Dustin and Raphael ran behind us.

Suddenly, my legs collapsed, and I crashed face-first into the asphalt. Once I hit the ground, shackles were slapped around my legs.

"Y'all get out of here!" I yelled to Nakia and the others as the White Dragon men gathered around me.

“You heard him! Let’s go call for help!” Raphael screamed.

“No! We are not leaving him!” Nakia yelled.

Dustin stood his ground and started throwing rocks at them. After covering up, Rocky yelled, “You’re a nigger-lover and a disgrace to the supreme race!”

They had a standoff while they kept eyes on each other, and everyone else stared at DeDe's corpse. Despite us not seeing eye to eye, I never wanted anything tragic to happen to him. My arms began trembling. Then purple rays blasted through my fingertips into the person Dustin was fussing with. His weapon was destroyed, and his group members were shook. Rocky yelled, "The experiment is activated! Beware of his Gamma rays!" They tried shooting at me, but my body was repellent to their attacks. I felt like a new man once the shackles fell off my feet.

Nakia tried tackling one of them, but he threw her to the group and pointed a dagger toward her neck, then said, "I'll kill you where you lay nigger-girl!"

At superhuman speed, I crashed my radioactive fist through the man’s stomach. He screamed as I felt his insides melt around my arm. My arms began glowing with purple energy.

Then I turned slowly. One of the other members charged me. I put my hands up for protection, and they sent purple light beam rays straight through his shoulder, cutting through his arm before severing half his body.

He used his dying breath to ask his friends to kill me. After watching their friend become dearly departed and my bulging purple arms, they ran off petrified.

When I looked up, Dustin and Raphael were petrified also, and Nakia was on the ground mourning over DeDe's dead body.

Chapter 18: The Gamma Cry

Dark clouds showered rain down on us as we gathered for DeDe's funeral. Everyone was dressed in all black, with their heads down and guarded by umbrellas. DeDe's father gave the eulogy. I could tell that DeDe came from a well-off family. It was sad to see him go out like that.

His father held himself together, which is more than I could say for most of us. DeDe's mom kept falling out and crying with an entourage around her across from the podium. This is how my mom must have been at Sinclair's services. It broke my heart twice that I wasn't able to attend his funeral.

It felt like she lost all her sons after Sinclair's death. I figured our relationship could never be the same, so I distanced myself from her. Some of that distance was beyond my control. I blamed her for what happened to Morris and my father.

Once I made it to the repast, Jessica appeared after placing her hands on my shoulder. I was caught off guard by her appearance at the services. When she told me DeDe's father was a politician, and I spotted her dad in the crowd, I eased my suspicion.

Regardless of Jessica's presence, I was scanning the event hall for Nakia, but she was nowhere to be found. My eyes settled on the Gammas. Antoine, Raphael Apollo, and Q prepared to lead a ritual the Gammas did for members at their funerals.

Once they finished, Senator Avery got on the microphone as usual and started lecturing, "I've known DeDorius's father for decades. He has been my friend and companion in my work and personal life. DeDe, as the community knew him, was an accomplished man in his own right. One of the outspoken leaders of Louisiana's oldest fraternity, Gamma Alpha Gamma. But make no mistake, my people. DeDorius' life was not lost in vain. This incident is the latest case of terrorism. This is a problematic issue, and we have been pushing the state of Louisiana to recognize it as a real threat to our society that warrants investigations nationwide. We will grow from this tragedy, so no more black men, women, boys, and girls need to die as a result of terrorism. You, as black people, have too much to fear from law enforcement and the evil people that those officers have sworn to protect you from. It stops now!"

I couldn't listen to this. I gently pushed his daughter away from me. She reached for me again, but I walked away with my hands in my pockets and my head down. When I looked up, I realized I had no choice but to encounter the Gammas. I tried greeting them and offering condolences, but they weren't trying to hear it. Antione said, "You can keep that apology. You were there when DeDe died. You could have done something, but let me guess, you weren't man enough to have your brother's back. That's nothing new."

Antoine pushed past me, Apollo shouldered me, and the rest of the Gammas followed behind them. I didn't think anyone except Jessica would be comfortable around me again. Unfortunately, my feelings about her changed, so I was all alone.

When I walked past the church, I heard someone call my name. The door was locked, but I managed to break through it. Dust was everywhere. Then I saw the back of someone in the front row of the church. I whispered Nakia's name while she drowned in her tears, with her head planted against her palms. When she spotted me, she exclaimed, "Go away!" Her demand echoed through the church.

I denied her request and comforted her, then said, “I wanted to check on you, but if you want to be alone, I could leave-” She grabbed my hand and said, “No, please stay.”

We stared into each other's eyes briefly before she started weeping again. I wrapped my arms around her and realized I was so focused on saving Morris that I forgot about Nakia. We needed each other.

She was the first person to express concern for what I went through. Our ability to make each other laugh during our hardest times spoke volumes about our connection. We shared a few laughs when I told her about somc of thc crazy things that happencd to me. I couldn't believe the last words Sinclair spoke came to life while I was captured. The vigilante group put the same fungi he was studying into my body. He was the only reason I knew about some of those terms. I wished I paid closer attention to his last words.

While I began giving in to my sorrows, Nakia said, "Cheer up, Gamma man!"

She seemed surprised when I told her I didn't think they would accept me back after Dede's death. Nakia proclaimed, “You did more than anyone. Dustin and Raphael were there. They can speak for you.”

I dropped my head and responded, "No, Nakia. I don't want them to. They still ain't really absorbed this whole situation by the looks of it, and I think I prefer it that way. That reminds me. Please don’t tell anybody about all this. My powers, the kidnapping. None of it. I’ll take care of those white dragons myself!”

Nakia whispered, “White Dragon. That’s who did all of this to you? That makes so much sense.”

Then she pulled out her phone, scrolled through random articles online, and continued, “The White Dragon was thought to be a myth. Generations of African American leaders sought to expose them, but no proof was ever brought to light. Because of the supernatural abilities and technology associated with the White Dragon, no self-respecting political figure would believe it. Forget this! They are about to believe it, and we will find Morris!”

I asked, “You don’t need time to mourn over DeDe?”

Nakia responded, "It's in our DNA to keep pushing through adversity."

Back at the ceremony, Nakia and I stood among the crowd as the rain continued to smother everyone. The last eulogy had just been given. The Gamma brothers stoodd around DeDe's coffin in hoods with their Greek letters.

"Gammas," Antoine howled.

"Man, oh man!" the Gammas echoed after him.

Each brother put his hand on the one next to him, and then they moved counterclockwise in a circle around DeDe's coffin.

"We lost a brother!" Antoine continued to lead the chant melodically.

"Man, oh man!"

"Prayers for his mother!"

"Man, oh man!"

"Was like no other!"

"Man, oh man!"

"We miss you brother!"

"Bye oh Bye!"

"We'll kiss your mother!"

"Hold her tight!"

"Life for another"

"Prayers up high!"

"Wings spread like butter!"

"Fly oh fly!"

"Farewell Oh brother!"

"Gammas Cry!"

Grief and feelings of helplessness came racing, boiling inside me. I couldn't help but think what it would feel like to be part of them. This was the greatest display of brotherhood I ever saw. I felt like a punk as tears came to my eyes, dropping from the purple gamma radiation that flickered in my pupils. This was the brotherhood I wanted and why I pledged Gamma. The was the brotherhood I longed for. Now, I could never have that with them. However, in two hours, Nakia and I would begin our quest to find my real brother.

Chapter 19: Finding Brother

I have never been more ready for anything in my life. Even driving through this hick part of Louisiana, I knew the road ahead wasn't going to be easy. Before we could reach our destination, Nakia began questioning me about Jessica. She still didn't know that she was one of her hero's daughters, and that night seemed like terrible timing to let her know. I'd never been happier to be lost once Nakia and I realized we had made a wrong turn. We decided to pull over at a gas station.

This gas station was like three truck stops put together. It had a mini-casino, a few restaurants, and a lot of in-and-out traffic. We spent more time than expected there, but we were happy to get back on track. Chill bumps began multiplying on my body the closer we got to our destination. I had a new concern once I noticed a car speeding in the rearview mirror. When I realized it was Apollo, I immediately noticed the vengeance on his face. He was going so fast that he rear-ended my vehicle while I was speeding.

Boom! The front bumper of Apollo's whip banged against the back of my whip and threw Nakia out of her sleep and seat. She wasn't buckled and bounced around the car like a ball in a pinball machine.

Once she held onto the headrest, she shouted, "Dago! He has a gun!"

Moments later, he shot out my back windshield. I have never seen such hatred on a man's face. His next shot took out my back tire. I lost control of the whip, and we were sent through the barricades and into the woods. Everything went black. When I regained consciousness, I began calling out for Nakia. She was still unconscious.

Boom! A shotgun bullet blasted the side of my car. I tucked Nakia's head into my chest for protection. I could barely breathe. Adrenaline rushed as my heart pounded.

"Come out Dago!" Apollo screamed as he let out another shot.

I shielded Nakia with my body after rolling from underneath the crashed car. I jumped out, clenched my fists, then screamed, "You want me, Apollo? Well, here I am!"

He yelled, "Let's get it then!" He pumped his shotgun one time. The confidence in his face faded once he saw my fists glowing. Before we attack each other, the White Dragon group emerged from the bushes. Once Nakia screamed, Rocky dove to the ground and jammed his gun against her head. Apollo dropped his weapon, and then we raised our hands.

Chapter 20: Brothers Through & Through

I was back chained to the floor in the woods across from Apollo. The ditch we were stuck in was locked by a steel gate and chained with a padlock. I kept apologizing but didn't get a response. He looked distraught and on the verge of giving up. I continued, "What's going on fool? You were so alive and ready to go when it was time to kill me. Now, all of a sudden, you're quiet? Nakia's in danger, and you don't give a damn."

His hazel eyes began watering, and he responded, "You are right, little bro. I don't give a damn about Nakia. You took everything I gave a damn about away from me. Maybe it's good you are suffering the way I did."

I ranted, "You really think I ain't suffer? I got kidnapped by these goons before, something I tried to tell y'all! I lost my brothers and everything I had going for me! I've suffered enough for all of us."

He clapped back, "That doesn't give you the right to make other people suffer!"

I didn't have a rebuttal for him. Both of us had our points, and fussing was the last thing we needed to do while our lives were in the hands of a vigilante group. Apollo asked, “Are these the clowns that killed DeDe?”

I nodded, then answered, "Yep, they killed DeDe, kidnapped Morris, and ran crazy experiments on me. Who knows what they are scheming on with Nakia? We have to get out of here and find her.”

“Psst… Dago.” A familiar voice whispered from above. I looked up, past the metal gate bars. Dustin and Raphael were calling for us alongside one another.

Our happiness faded away when I saw how defeated Apollo was. I signaled for them to hide once a hooded man appeared. He looked at Apollo and said, "You are as good as a dead boy." Then he turned to me and said, "Now, you are the nigger we need."

After he unlocked the gate, Raphael punched him in the back of the head. While he yelled in anguish, Raphael took the chain from him and wrapped it around his neck. After he took his last breath, his mask fell off. I was shook when I saw it was a man I saw at the gas station.

Raphael lifted me to my feet. I felt energy jolting through my body. Once I reiterated that we needed to find Nakia, Raphael gestured toward Apollo and asked, "What about him?"

Dustin said, "Let him die. He tried to kill Dago!"

"But he's a Gamma man," Raphael said.

We thought Apollo was almost to the upper room before he gasped, "Leave me here to die. My life ain't worth living."

Dustin kept urging us to leave him for dead. Apollo couldn't believe his eyes when he saw me advocating for him. I convinced them to help him out since he was their Gamma brother. That sentiment got through to them. I gently grabbed the keys from Raphael's hand before walking over to Apollo. I got down on one knee and unchained him. Dustin tried to step toward me, but Raphael blocked him with an arm.

Apollo cried out, "Why did you save me? I was just trying to kill you."

I quickly responded, "You're their Gamma big brother. That's how they should be there for their Gamma brothers regardless of what y'all go through."

He used me to leverage himself off the ground. When we were face to face, he said, "I'm not just their Gamma brother. I'm your Gamma brother too! We are part of the Gamma Beta Family. The most storied family in the Gamma Alpha Gamma Fraternity!"

Chapter 21: Together United

Footsteps tracked through the mud as I led the Gammas through the wetland terrain of the White Dragon hideout. We moved swiftly but discretely. The groups of White Dragon goons we passed were telling racist jokes, chewing tobacco, and shining their weapons.

Once we reached high ground, I called the Gammas to a halt and said, "I think they're keeping her at the base lobby. It looks like some kind of offices are in there. That's where they keep their plans and important documents."

Dustin interjected, "Nah Dago. They are keeping her in another ditch somewhere like they had y'all."

I thought about it for a few seconds and responded, "Maybe, but it can take hours to run around in the dark, looking for ditches. The base lobby down there is one bright place. We should check there first to make the best use of time." Dustin and I looked at Apollo and Raphael for their thoughts.

Apollo answered, "I don't disagree that we might be better served hitting the base first."

Raphael contrarily interjected, "But that's suicide. We would go in there, knowing we have a high probability of dying."

I squeezed the mud in my hand until it oozed out between the cracks of my fingers and proclaimed, "That's a risk I'm willing to take." Suddenly, I heard murmurs and chatters as a small crew of White Dragon members walked our way. All of us hit the ground and crawled under the bushes in a synchronized motion.

Raphael whispered, "I have an idea. We have something they don't - Gamma power. Let's walk into their trap and take over. Dago, we should follow your lead in there. If any of them gets out of line, put your powers to use, and we will have your back."

I felt fire and adrenaline rushing through my veins when I saw the opportunity to get revenge and get closer to saving the woman I love. The most unfit one in the group was by himself with his back turned. We emerged from the bushes, and I put him in a chokehold. Raphael knocked out the first person who reacted and took his gun. The fight began to even out once one of the White Dragons threw Dustin through the ground. When the other crew stepped in and tried jumping him, I put my powers to use. They were on their back and begging for mercy before they could lay another hand on him.

Only one person was coherent enough to talk. He yelled, "The experiment! How did you escape?" I wanted to ask them where Nakia was, but I felt my life in danger when they began yelling and looking for their weapons. I left all of them lifeless, but our problems weren't over.

Once they were silenced, we heard two other White Dragon members patrolling. "Let's take their outfits!" I exclaimed. We grabbed the masks, capes, armor, and robes of the White Dragon crew and dragged their naked bodies into the bushes.

"Everything alright here, 315?" A patroller asked.

I was silent until I realized that the numbers they called were out on my chest. I mimicked his voice and responded, "Yes."

Before they had time to realize we weren't who they thought we were, a siren sounded. The patrollers pumped their fists and exclaimed, "He's here!" We trailed behind the White Dragon men as they shuffled through the dense mud. As we walked down the hill, it all got real. I saw a familiar nightmare. The scary sight of White Dragon goons gathered at the base. There were at least 50 of them.

Before long, we were standing among the goons. I felt the anxiety from the Gammas start emerging and the energy in the air shifting. Then, a fleet of vehicles arrived. The first truck pulled up, and all the White Dragon men raised their guns. We followed suit.

The truck doors opened, and Rocky and the captain exited the vehicle. The two men who put me through so much misery that my spine curled by putting eyes on them. As they walked close to us, my hands shivered. I felt the Gamma energy building up. My shivers became uncontrollable when the captain called out Apollo for being out of line.

He said, "Discipline is lacking here, I see. I must note that I need to provide some additional training for this sector."

Then he paused and asked Rocky, "Is everyone accounted for?"

He answered, "There is no sign of 260. He was the one helping guard the niggers we captured."

The captain raised his voice and said, "Find him now! Make sure the experiment is neutralized with the offset device so his powers are mitigated. What about the other blacks we found? Where are they? They need to be killed on sight!"

Rocky answered, "Yes sir! We'll get on it. The colored girl is about to arrive." Moments later, a mysterious van pulled up. Once Nakia was dragged out of the back of the van, my blood began boiling. She was drugged, and her mouth was taped. Nakia had been zapped of her strength and tortured just like me.

Once Nakia got within arm's reach of the captain, he choked her and yelled, "Where are they?"

When she didn't respond, he smacked her. Blood rushed to my face, and then my weapon blew up in my hand. My costume disintegrated with purple energy waves.

"The experiment! Kill him!" The Captain yelled.

Chapter 22: The Gamma Melody

The whole camp was in flames and a wasteland within seconds. I ran through the mud, nearly naked. Nakia was wrapped in my arms as I sprinted past dead White Dragon bodies. Corpses littered the wetland. The Captain yelled, "Capture them!"

He chased after me with three other White Dragon goons. Suddenly, I lost my footing. A boomerang slashed my ankles, and then I stumbled to the ground. Nakia rolled away from me. As I turned around, ready to let a gamma ray loose, the Captain threw something into my chest.

I was hit with a stabilizer, and my gamma radiation was neutralized.

The Captain jumped on top of me and shoved his knee into my throat. Then he yelled, “You were a fool to attack my men, boy! If you weren’t so valuable, I would kill you now!”

He yanked Nakia off the ground and put a dagger on her neck, then said, “I don’t need her, boy! So, I’m going to make you watch as I carve her up like a turkey on Thanksgiving?"

"Drop it!" One of the White Dragon men yelled.

Two of them drew their weapons at the Captain. The second person shot the Captain in the leg. I thought I was next to die.

One of them slowly removed the device from my chest so I could breathe again. After I was helped to my feet, Raphael and Dustin removed their masks.

The Captain yelled, "Take those uniforms off! You can't wear them! They are for White Dragons only!"

I put a weapon to his head, then demanded, "Tell me where Morris is right now before you're a corpse like the rest of the White Dragons."

I knew weakening the Captain wouldn't be an easy task. As I contemplated my next move, I heard a buzzing. "Y'all hear that?" Raphael asked.

It's getting closer, like a bee in my ear. "D Dub, watch out!" Dustin yelled.

While we ducked for cover, the Captain got away on a mini-aircraft. He flew away with my hopes of finding Morris. I couldn't return to everyday life empty-handed and without my big brother.

Nakia was still drugged, but I seemed to be the only one who cared. I felt the side eyes from my brothers while I tried nursing her back to health.

I couldn't help but feel like a failure. I put my fraternity brothers in a messed-up situation for personal reasons. Nakia was in this condition because of what I dragged her in. And for what? There was no headway on finding Morris.

"What's that? It's blinking!" Dustin asked as he picked up a mini cell phone and threw it to me.

A message with coordinates appeared on the screen. It gave the location and mapping of a moving target. The number 5 flashed on the screen.

"Wait, you ain't thinking about following him, huh?" Dustin asked.

I took a deep breath and responded, "I don't have a choice, man. I came out here to find my brother. This is the only clue I have.

When they tried following me, I pleaded for them to take care of Nakia. Dustin and Raphael showed me that our brotherhood was deeper than the fraternity when they showed they were willing to put everything on the line for me. Despite their desire to join, this was something I had to accomplish by myself. Once my brothers wouldn't let me turn down their assistance, I said, “Follow the trail back to the White Dragon camp and steal one of their whips. Hurry before the others come. We killed most of them clowns, but it won’t be long before the rest come to investigate.”

“We ain’t losing another Gamma”, Raphael said.

“I ain’t no Gamma no more. But I am your brother. And I love y’all.”

“*Brothers*”, Raphael started melodically. I would have called him corny any other time, but truth be told, I was so wound up in emotion, I felt like a cornball myself.

“We Gamma Brothers”, Dustin joined.

“Brothers…. We Gamma Pride”, they both sang the forbidden Gamma melody that only brothers ears were privy to. *“Brothers, there’s no one other…. Brothers we love to vibe.”*

“And Brothers… I love my brother.”

“My brother is my life”.

“Gamma Brothers live!”

“Love, love being a…. Love, love being a…. Love, I love being a…. Gamma Alpha Gamma Brother”

I took a step back and teared up. Although I never heard the song in full, I knew all the words as they came. I felt my heart sink into the pits of the deepest mine any white supremacist could've buried me in. Any fraternity pledge master could've had me fight my own pledge brother in. It all came full circle when I saw my brothers embrace me.

The Gammas and Nakia pushed forward, and within minutes, they were gone. I disguised myself using whatever clothes I could rip from the White Dragons. Stepping over dead bodies in the cold, foggy, and muddy swamp intensified the mission.

I followed the bodies of water to the path the map led me to. The green light turned red the closer I got. The '5' flashed faster. I was closing in. I moved quick enough to catch up to him, but slow enough to conserve my energy.

I felt the gamma radiation within me. The closer I got, the stronger I got. Once I closed in on my target, the phone died.

I was fuming until I heard something moving in the bushes. I maneuvered through dense vegetation and followed the sounds leading to a floodplain. Once I was at the edge of the bushes, a familiar voice said, "You came to find me baby! My Prince Charming!"

Chapter 23: Barbie's Dreamboat

My legs began trembling once I saw Jessica at a boat dock. I was suspicious about her appearing, but I was more concerned about charging the device. When I began asking about her outlets and chargers on board, she brought up how distant I've been from her. Getting along with her while she was mad at me stood in the way of finding my brother, so I had to play along. Once I told her I apologized, she started charging the device.

My mind was eased when I saw several other boats cruise by, but I began getting antsy when the device took a prolonged amount of time to come back on. While I prayed for the phone to hurry up and turn on, Jessica said, "Fate brought you here to me, and fate will make you stay. Are you joining Daddy and I for dinner?" I figured her father would be able to help me since he always preached about hate crimes and terrorism.

I felt ever more out of place when Senator Avery called my name as he stood surrounded by several politicians. He ran down the line of all politicians I should call my people, but were they my people? These negroes seemed so happy just to be alongside the whites. They felt cold and distant from the struggle, aside from DeDe's father.

He caressed my elbow while shaking my hand and said, "I recognize you from DeDe's funeral. You all weren't close, were you?"

I responded, "He was my pledge master."

The Senator proudly added, "Dagobert, here is a Gamma and member of Louisiana's finest fraternity."

A politician I recognized named Harvey interjected, "That's not what I heard from DeDorius before he tragically passed away. He told me you were expelled some time ago."

Once I confirmed the rumor, everyone looked disappointed except for Harvey. He looked at me with the same type of hate and disgust that the White Dragons did. It was like he expected the worst out of me.

Revisiting my expulsion from the Gammas killed me inside. And to hear Harvey speak those words belittled me. The ghost of DeDe haunted me by reminding me that I'm not Gamma material and not worthy of brotherhood.

Truth be told, I knew I wasn't Gamma material. What I did to Apollo was foul, and I deserved expulsion. However, just because I wasn't worthy of being a Gamma didn't mean I wasn't worthy of brotherhood. I loved my Gamma homies like my own brothers, but there was a time and place for unconditional love. In this moment, I was reminded of the only brotherhood that mattered to me at the time - Morris.

Once the other men pivoted and began discussing something else, as I wasn't there, I said, "Senator, I need to speak to you in private."

He whispered, "Meet me on the other side of the deck in a few minutes. I need to have a quick word with these fine gentlemen, and I'll talk with you after."

While waiting on the other side of the dock, I noticed a drop of blood on the deck floor. I began tracing a trail of dots while my heart dropped at the sight of each consecutive drop. The blood trail led me to Rocky slumped in a corner where he could go unseen.

I began counting down until I killed him if he didn't tell me where Morris was. When I got to one, he begged, "Okay, I'll tell you. Please don't kill me! I'll tell you! I'll tell you!"

Before he could tell me, someone yelled, "What the heck is all of this?"

While I pinned my knee deeper into Rocky's neck, I said, "Senator, this is what I wanted to tell you about. This monster snuck onto your boat, and he is part of a terrorist white supremacy group."

The Senator looked at Rocky and asked, "Is this true, Owen?"

Rocky adhered to the name Owen but avoided answering the question.

The Senator's face was filled with embarrassment and pity. I took my knee off Rocky's neck, then Senator Avery kneeled by Rocky and said, "Dagobert, Owen is my son. His face is a reflection of me but not my views of your people."

I wondered, "How could someone so 'righteous' and so proud of his commitment to black people breed a piece of crap like this. I couldn't believe it and refused to believe it." Biting my tongue wasn't an option. I said,

"I'm sorry, Senator, but your son is a terrorist. He knows where his vigilante group is keeping my brother."

The Senator stood up, rubbed his eyebrows, and said, "Oh, this is so troubling. Does anybody else know about this? Have they seen Owen's face?" I shrugged to maintain my leverage.

Senator Avery's anger turned his face the color of beets. He kneeled back down and demanded Rocky tell him where Morris was. Rocky immediately handed his father a tracking device with coordinates to Morris's location. Senator Avery said, "Dagobert if you're going to find your brother, you will need a SWAT team by your side. You will need the police. Hell, you'll need the got damn Louisiana state militia. These white supremacist terrorists cannot be taken lightly. I am going to provide you with the militia, all the police you need, and the force of the SWAT team. You're going to use these coordinates to find your brother, but in return, I need something from you."

I reached a new level of bravery when I told him, "I can't promise you that."

He showed his force and ability to be ruthless when he responded, “If the identity of my son is revealed that he is a member of a dangerous White Supremacist organization, it will ruin me. I need you to promise this won’t get out.” I maintained my stance. Then he continued, “You’re going to have to promise me this if you ever want to see your brother again.” I gave him my word, and we shook on it. Once he felt secure, he handed me the tracking device and said, “I will put you in contact with all the militia and police forces you will need. They will pick you up via helicopter in an hour.”

Regardless of my word, I could tell that the Senator didn't trust it. We stared at each other for several seconds, then he said, "On second thought." Before I could ask him what he was referring to, he pulled a gun out of his waistband and emptied the clip into Rocky's chest.

Chapter 24: Morris

The wind blasted my face from hundreds of feet in the air. We were so high in the sky that my skin was frozen solid. "We're almost there, son," an officer wearing a breathing mask and SWAT gear said as he gripped my shoulder.

Another officer said, "We've pinpointed the coordinates as much as possible." Then he grabbed a parachute sealed in a bag, pressed it against my boy's chest, and said, "Suit up, brother!" Before I could respond, he prepared me to jump off the helicopter. He forced my arms through the straps of the parachute bag and tightened it on me while standing with his back to the open helicopter door. Once I prepared, he yelled, "Once we touch the ground, follow my signal!"

He was out of the plane before I could respond. I looked out the door and saw the horrific sight of woods from a distance. The pilot convinced me to jump by saying, "You might want to go before you lose the others."

"For Morris," I whispered, then jumped.

Gravity took control of me, pulling my body as it raced toward the earth in free fall. My insides were in shambles, and I feared these were my final moments on earth. My fear vanished once I heard a pop, and my free fall slowed down. The noise pulled me backward with a calming force, and I felt the parachute push open. It caught the wind and allowed me to glide down at ease.

Dawn just broke through, with the sun barely poking from the clouds, as I floated down to my feet. We were in the middle of nowhere – exactly the type of place I assumed the White Dragons were hiding Morris.

Once I landed, I was surrounded by police and state militia, all dressed in SWAT gear. They began following me once I called out the coordinates on the tracker. When we began making progress, the tracker began beeping chaotically. The tracker made it seem as if we reached our destination, but Morris was nowhere in sight.

I spazzed as I shoved the tracker into the dirt. The gamma radiation emitted from my hand as I punched it into the earth, blowing up the tracker. Several law enforcement members began spazzing also once I destroyed the tracker. One of their leaders said, "Relax, relax, gentlemen! We'll figure it out together. Let's search the perimeter."

As he gave the command, I felt the ground pulse beneath me. I could hear it living like a heartbeat. When the gamma waves emitted from my blood, they sent signals through the earth that bounced back to me. I was communicating with it and nature. It was telling me something, so I fell to my knees. My body began vibrating, and veins in my head slithered, flushing an overload of blood through my face. The skin on my hands bubbled, and then I squeezed down to rip into the grass.

My vision went purple, clouded by the flush of gamma waves in my blood. I could see every particle of air and every element of gas, oxygen, nitrogen, and hydrogen. They formed a path for me to connect with something else - another energy source emitting gamma waves right back at me.

I yelled Morris's name, then felt a gravitational pull thirty feet away from me. "Follow him!" The SWAT leader yelled. A road of gamma signatures formed in my vision. The gamma path led me to a spot in the woods where I felt intense radiation. It was underneath the earth, pulling for me. When I stared down, I saw gamma waves shaped into a man curled in a fetal position underground.

"He's down here!" I yelled.

My fist pulsed from the gamma waves and formed a shield of purple energy around it. I punched into the ground, barely cracking it. Then, I punched enough to break through it again and again. I kept punching, breaking away rock and crust from the earth as I dug for my big brother.

I quickly pulled through the rock that sealed him underground. I was able to excavate him from the earth, but he wasn't breathing. "Help!" I screamed. The medic quickly rushed to his aid and pushed down on Morris's chest.

The chest pumps weren't working, so I began panicking and praying. His body jumped three times, but his eyes remained shut. I closed my eyes, too, and then a gamma wave rushed down my arms, through my hands, and into Morris's chest. My eyes lit up light like New Year's fireworks once Morris awakened.

Chapter 25: My Brother's Keeper

A banner reading 'Welcome Home Morris' was spread across the top of the Gamma Alpha Gamma fraternity mansion. Morris' composite photo was printed, blown up, and promoted throughout the event. A poolside cookout and women from every sorority added to the special vibe. Everyone Gamma from the past decade was at the party.

I hadn't seen that many happy people in one place for years. It reminded me of how terrible the last couple of years of my life had been. However, with those reminders came the joy of allowing happiness to flourish in its own space again.

I placed my hand on Morris's shoulder and asked, "What do you think, family?" as he sat in his wheelchair from the balcony of the Gamma house, observing the crowd that attended to honor him.

It pained me to see him like this – weak, fragile, and crippled. Back in his day, Morris was bigger and stronger than me and an athlete in every sense of the word. He was a fraternal man and a champion.

Someone the gammas proudly promoted as theirs. They all saw his return as a gift from heaven.

Antione approached Q and said, "What are you doing here, Dora Winifred? This is a Gamma function. Even though we made it an open guest list, expelled members aren't allowed on the Gamma Alpha Gamma property. I'm afraid I'm going to have to ask you to vacate the premises."

After all the lengths I went through to find my big brother, this was the last thing I wanted to happen. This wasn't the time and place for him to know about my lowest moments since he'd been gone. Everything Morris said that night had been a whisper until he said, "Brother Antione, what gives you the right to speak to my flesh and blood like that?"

Antione smirked and said, "What gives me the right is that your brother is a snake. He likes going around and hooking up with his pledge master's girlfriends. Morris, you're a Gamma legend, but your brother isn't Gamma material. There's a rule in the Gamma rulebook that says 'expelled members aren't allowed on Gamma Grounds. With that being said, Dora Winifred is an expelled member, so he cannot be here."

Morris positioned his body in the wheelchair so Antoine could see his chest, then responded, "I hear you, but to be clear – my brother is no snake, and you will watch your mouth when discussing my family. Also, if you'd like to bring up the rules, don't manipulate them. Article b15 on the bottom half of page 58 states – If a member is expelled from the Gamma fraternity, they aren't allowed on Gamma grounds unless their blood relative is in the Gamma Hall-of-Fame. Surely you know this, Antoine, or has my beloved fraternity elected a president who neglected to read and comprehend the bylaws? Have we fallen off that hard?"

"Of course, I know the bylaws, my brother. It's great to have you back, Morris, and of course, your brother can stay," Antoine answered angrily. He quickly shook off his emotions and faked a smile as authentic as cubic zirconia earrings.

Before they could walk off, Morris asked, "Do you ever wish you could've stayed with the Gammas?" Antione and Q eagerly awaited my answer. Morris reiterated my questions after a few moments of awkward silence.

Antione and I locked eyes, and then I answered, “Of course I do.

He drilled back, “What do you regret missing out on the most? The prestige? The clout? The women? The parties?”

Morris was in the midst of fulfilling the father role he once filled. Without tears, I cried out, “The brotherhood! There isn’t anything I wanted more! Forget the women, clout, and prestige. I already had that. I just wanted the brotherhood. I told y’all when I came here that I was willing to put the blood, sweat, and tears into this fraternity.”

Morris proudly said, "You hear that, Mr. President? That’s a good brother right there. He knows plenty about brotherhood! Maybe not with the Gamma Alpha Gamma, but with me and those other Gamma brothers right there.” When my line brothers approached and insinuated Morris’s point, he became infuriated.

The tension was thicker than fog. Antione and Morris were used to being the top dog, but Morris showed his dominance in front of others. It seemed like only the end of a battle, not the war. The tension wasn't diffused until someone began speaking on the microphone.

Nakia's voice took over the party when she said, "Attention, brothers of the great Gamma Alpha Gamma Fraternity. Today, we celebrate the homecoming of one of the most accomplished brothers of your fraternity! Morris Waller's legacy with the Gammas speaks for itself. When Morris went to school here, he was an established community organizer, accomplished athlete, and a distinguished scholar."

She looked and sounded captivating as she stood at the front of the lawn. Nakia stood proud and beautiful, and I reflected on how brave this woman was. She stood by my side when I needed her and put herself in harm's way for a cause she was passionate about.

Behind her towered the man who inspired her. Others looked at him like a hero, but I couldn't look at him the same anymore. The days of looking up to him were long gone. When we locked eyes, he acted as if everything else was the same. I wondered what else he was covering up.

Nakia continued about Morris's accomplishments and accolades, but everything sounded like background noise until Dustin gripped my shoulder and asked if I was okay. I lied and said I was fine. Things couldn't be fine until I talked more with Morris. After he finished receiving his flowers, I asked, "What all happened to you big brother? We never really got into everything that took place." He continued to stance of – he forgot. However, when Morris lied, he tapped his right foot. When he saw me watching his right foot tapping, he knew he couldn't keep it a secret much longer.

Once he was about to respond, Nakia came back on the microphone and said, "Today is a day we celebrate our good brother Morris, but let's not forget the threat of White Supremacy and the threat of the White Dragon - the most dangerous terrorist organization of our time. This vigilante group threatens the very existence of black and brown folks in America. We need to mobilize, analyze, and strategize for war with this enemy, but for today… let's enjoy the celebration and camaraderie."

I let Morris have his day, but I still wanted answers. Q and Antione were still standing by us after Nakia's speech. Q told Antione, “There’s still no sign of Apollo. The police have been looking everywhere.”

Antione loudly whispered, “Do not tell the brothers until we find out what happened to him.”

A soft, warm hand rubbed my neck, and then a sweet voice asked, "Why don't you seem happy?"

I answered, “How could I be? After everything we went through. Yeah, I’m glad to have Morris back, but what about the White Dragon? They are still out there.”

She compassionately said, “Maybe, but we will fight them, my brother.”

As much as I loved brotherhood, I hated it when Nakia referenced it. That wasn’t for me and her, and I thought that was clear by now. I didn’t want there to be any confusion regarding how I felt about her.

I said, “Nakia, look. I need to tell you someth -”

I didn’t like Senator Avery even more when he interrupted me and said, “Nakia, you were great up there! You are really becoming a politician.”

She smiled and responded, "Thank you, Senator! I'm not so sure that's a good thing, but I'll accept it coming from you." The Senator sensed my anger and then asked to speak to me alone.

He shrouded me with his wingspan, then asked, "What did you think of your brother's welcome home event?"

I got straight to the point and said, "You killed your own son. All to protect your political career."

He shielded me with his body and forced us away from everyone, then asked, "Would you prefer if I let him live? A white supremacist terrorist, hell-bent on killing black folks."

I responded, "I know what he was, but he was still your son. You raising a kid like that makes me question a lot about you. But the fact that you killed him to salvage your reputation says even more."

The Senator stepped toward me and asked, "Is that the thanks I get for helping you find your brother?"

It took an effort for me to push his heavy arm off my shoulder. He responded by surrendering and saying, "Alright, Dagobert. I hoped to keep this all a secret, but if you know this much, you should know it all. The truth is, I had suspected that Owen was a racist for some time. Many things were wrong with that boy, but that's not important. What is important is that his secret affairs led me to investigate exactly what he was up to. I had done some in-depth investigation with the help of law enforcement. The White Dragon is more dangerous than we initially thought. They're one of the most lethal terrorist organizations across the globe with a ruthless leader called The Grand Dragon."

When he said The Grand Dragon, it instantly took me back to the lab where my Gamma powers were born. I heard the White Dragon devils speak that name before. I remembered the White Dance, the hordes of White Dragon goons, and the giant that sat among them. Could that have been The Grand Dragon? Gamma rays began brewing through my blood as I reflected, and while Morris, Dustin, and Raphael approached. Senator Avery acknowledged them, then looked at me and said, "I'm glad you found your brother, Dagobert. But the truth is, we have so much more we need to do. There is a war coming, and you'll need brotherhood to survive it."

www.ingramcontent.com/pod-product-compliance
Lightning Source LLC
Chambersburg PA
CBHW070618310726
48982CB00001B/112

* 9 7 9 8 9 9 0 6 1 8 1 8 3 *